CONFUSION:
Till Drugs and Death Do Us Part

BY NORM SALTER

xulon PRESS

INTRODUCTION

In the world we live in, at least for the past 20 years, households have come to rely on two incomes to survive. Both parents have to work in order to make enough money to provide for their families. Most of us seem to fall into the habit of trying to raise our children the same way we were raised. Unfortunately, that doesn't work because the world around us changes all the time. Today's children are exposed to more and more things we never imagined when we were kids. I myself tried to raise my two older children the way I was raised. It was a disaster. The sad reality is that nowadays children are more on their own than earlier times in history.

I have heard many young adults say that they raised themselves, and was just given a place to eat and sleep. Some parents send their kids off to school, expect the teachers will raise their kids, and hope for the best. When my wife and I were raising our two older children the drug problem was just beginning to escalate in our country, and by the 1980's drug use was rampant. We didn't realize the ugly truth until it was too late. The school our two older kids attended was a haven of drugs and violence. On the up side, my wife and I got a second chance. We had another child many years later, when we were older, and learned how to be better parents than we were to first two kids.

I wrote this book based on real life experiences I have witnessed over the years as a parent, contractor, and a coach of both boys and girls sports. I listened to other parents who were struggling with their children. I want adults to see the world from a teenager's perspective. Adults need to see how children survive raising themselves. Furthermore, what they will do to manage their stress by using drugs, and what they will risk to get drugs when addiction sets in. The sad conclusion is that by the time most parents realize what is happening to their drug addicted children, it's far too late to intervene.

I hope the story will help parents with young children and teenagers have a different outlook and find ways to communicate better with their children. I hope parents will understand the importance of strong relationships and trust with their children, because that is what really counts. Love and trust can conquer a multitude of potential problems, but it takes invested time and sincerity to get there. Are you willing to make that journey? Or, are you willing to accept the results of your absence?

ACKNOWLEDGMENTS

**With much appreciation and a
Big Thank You to:**

All those who helped me with this book.

Jeannie, my wife who has Parkinson 's disease,
through all her pain spent many hours correcting
and typing and retyping. Without her sacrifice,
the book would have never been written.

Sallie, my youngest daughter, who came
forward with her expertise. She really helped
pull it all together in the final stages and got it
to completion for printing.

Evey Grice, for her gifts and talents

To the many friends who have encouraged me.

Any others that I may have forgotten who
helped me with this book.

CHAPTER 1

There was a slight breeze and the air was crisp on that early spring morning as John Colden walked home from work. John was a very tall, handsome and robust man with a quiet manner and very confident about himself. He worked the midnight shift at a factory making automobile parts and only lived about two miles away. As he walked along whistling, he thought about the events of his life over the past two years since his first wife died, leaving him with two daughters, Amber, now 17 years old, and Kim, 15.

He married again a year after his wife passed. Shortly after, he realized he married out of loneliness and had made a grave mistake. His new wife, Vickie, was not the sweet, innocent woman she pretended to be before he married her. Reality set in quickly, as the rudeness and nasty temper was revealed. The harsh way she treated his two girls was so over bearing, he quickly changed his thoughts and began thinking about the happy days with his first wife, Carol. He remembered the first time he met her as she came running down the street with her long hair flying behind her. She was late for an appointment, which he could not remember now, but all he could remember is that when she came around the corner, she ran into him, knocking him to the ground as she fell on top of him. Her beauty stunned him, for she was the prettiest thing he had ever laid eyes on. John realized quickly he was much older than Carol, but he couldn't help himself from being embarrassed as he helped her up. She couldn't take her eyes off him either; she thought he was the best looking guy she had ever seen.

An immediate spirit of love kindled and they both felt it. He very shyly asked her if he could walk her home. Under any other circumstances she would have said no to a perfect stranger, but this was different. She had a good instinctive feeling it would be all right; she did not want to lose contact with him, so she said yes, it will be all right. "Thank you," John replied. As they walked and talked, they got to know each other better adding to their attraction. When they reached Carol's house she invited him in to meet her parents. At first they were apprehensive about John because of how much older he was than Carol, but as they talked and got to know him better, they realized he was a good man and it would be alright.

A few months later, they were happily married and they loved each other very much. The one thing John adored about Carol was how she was so full of compassion, wisdom, and understanding. She was so full of life, she never saw anything wrong in the people around her, she only saw the good, and never the bad. Oh, how he loved her. He just couldn't see how God could let this happen to them, for she died just at the most important time in their lives, with two young girls;

John desperately needed her wisdom in raising them.

Reality quickly set back in as John rounded the corner to his home. He could hear the yelling and the screaming coming from inside the house, from his wife Vickie, Amber, and Kim. Vickie's lungs were at peak performance as she hollered out nasty words and threats, at the girls. He quickly ran up the steps, opened the door, and entered. It became suddenly quiet as all three of them stared at John. Then Molly, the family dog, barked and ran to John, wagging her tail and jumping on him, she was always so happy to see him. In the meantime they were all waiting to hear what he was going to say.

John's eyes roamed the room as he looked at them and then he finally said in a quiet voice, "All right, what's the matter this time?"

He had no more gotten the words out of his mouth when they all started screaming and talking at the same time. He threw his hands in the air and yelled for quiet; the room became silent again. He looked at Vickie and said, "What's the problem?"

Vickie quickly jumped on her soapbox and said, "I can't get them to do anything around here. I give them jobs to do and they won't do them. When you're not here you don't know the trouble they give me."

At that point both the girls started shouting, "That's not true! That's a lie!" John again yelled quiet, and it became silent again. He slowly walked across the room where the girls were standing. Amber had a hard stony look in her eyes and her jaw was tight as she was holding her anger in. Kim was crying as she looked up at her father. He reached out and with a smile gently ran his hand through her hair. He realized at that moment she was so much like Carol. She had the same gentleness, beauty and personality. He also realized it was being destroyed. Amber was harder for him to understand. She had a mental toughness that Kim didn't have, and she kept things inside. She wouldn't confide in him like Kim would. There was a mystery about Amber he just couldn't unravel, but one thing he knew for sure; no one was going to walk on her because she was a scrapper. She had to be, the city they lived in was a tough place to survive. The schools were bad. Drugs and alcohol were rampant, with almost no control. There were some good teachers, but a lot of bad ones as well.

John spoke up then, "You girls better get to school; it's getting late."

As the girls headed out the door, Kim turned and looked at her father and said, "Daddy, would you walk a ways with me so I can talk to you?"

Vickie glared at her with hatred, not daring to say anything.

They walked out of the house and across the street to take a short cut through the park in their neighborhood. As they reached the park, Kim stared down at the ground. "Daddy, why did you marry that woman?"

John reached out and touched her on the shoulder as they stopped walking. He looked around and then said, "Let's go sit on the bench over there and talk."

They walked over and as they sat down, he said, "Honey, a man can get very lonely without a woman in his life, and there are certain needs he has that only a woman can give."

"Well, you have Amber and me," Kim said in a raised voice.

"But that's not the same," he said with a smile. "When you get older, I'll try to explain it to you."

"I'm old enough," said Kim. She looked at John for a moment and said, "Does it have to do with sex?"

John looked at her with a startled expression and stuttering slowly, he said, "Well, yes, that's part of it." They were both silent for a moment and then John said, "I promise you, honey, I'm going to do something about these problems. We can't go on like we have been. You better get to school. I'll talk to you again later."

Kim jumped up and took off running, and then suddenly she stopped, went back and kissed him on the cheek, then headed for school. As she ran, her hair flying behind her, she reminded him even more of Carol.

Amber was almost to school as she passed an old building that should have been torn down a long time ago. Suddenly she heard someone whistle a tune she recognized. She looked around to see if anyone was watching and then darted into the building. There Jake stood, smiling, as she came up to him. Jake was a tall young man about 19 years old who had been kicked out of school a few years back for possession of drugs. He was quite handsome.

"Where ya been?" he asked, as she walked around him in a teasing way.

"I had another run in with that woman my dad calls his wife," she explained. "Boy, I hate her with a passion. She tells lies to my dad about Kim and me. I can't figure her out...it's like she's hiding something and afraid we're gonna find out."

Jake took some cocaine out of his pocket, took a sniff and handed it to Amber. She took a sniff and as she handed it back, she said, "I'm sure glad you can afford this stuff, I'm so broke."

Jake smiled and took her in his arms and said, "Honey, as long as you give me what I want, it'll always be here."

Amber looked up into his eyes and said, "I'll always be here." She put her arms around his neck and kissed him and scampered off to school.

Amber was now late for school. She rushed to her locker, grabbed her books and fled to her first class. As she entered the room and sat down, she received a stern look from her teacher, Mrs. Turner. She was a tall, slim woman with a coarse voice when she spoke.

"Amber, this is the third time you've been late this week, I'm going to have to send you to the principal's office and you can tell him your problems. I give up."

Amber got up, slowly walked down the hall to the principal's office, went in and sat down in the first chair she saw.

The secretary, Mrs. Conklin, looked at her and said, "Well, I see you're back again." Mrs. Conklin was a short, husky woman who spoke with a very tough attitude to the students, to cover up any fear she might have of them. "You must like us a lot to want to spend so much time in our office. What did you do this time?"

Amber made a face then turned her head away and didn't answer.

The principal, Mr. Frazer, came out of his office, handed his secretary some papers, and instructed her in what he wanted her to do with them. He was a tall, slender man with a nice smile, and had more patience with his students than most of his staff. He never lost his cool and always tried to stay calm, no matter what the situation was. He looked up, saw Amber, and stood looking at her silently for a moment. "Come into my office, Amber," he said as he held the door for her.

Amber stormed into his office, and sat down hard in a chair. Mr. Frazer walked into his office behind her. His eyes never left her as she stomped her feet, like keeping time to music from or nerves, and rolled her eyes around the ceiling with a very disgusted look on her face, wishing she were somewhere else. She was angry and it showed. As he sat down, he picked up a pencil and a piece of paper. Then he said as he looked at her again, "Amber, I could write a note to your father, but would it really do any good? You know, I've known your father a long time. We grew up together in this town, did a lot of things together when we were young. You used to be a fine student but the past couple of years, since your mother passed away; you seem to be going the wrong way. You just don't seem to have any spark to you anymore. Is there anything I can do to help you?"

Amber just said, "Write the letter and let me out of here. I need to go."

"No," he said, "I won't write it this time, but if it happens again I'll have to. Is there anything I can do to help you? Is there anything I can do?"

"No, I just want to go," Amber repeated.

"All right," Mr. Frazer said, "you may go, but let me give you some advice. I saw you with that young fellow, Jake — you know who I'm talking about. I've seen you with him a couple of times. He's trouble and he'll take you right along with him. Take it for what it's worth, but you really should stay away from him."

Amber looked at him angrily and told him, "It's none of your business what I do when I'm not on the school grounds. I do what I want."

Mr. Frazer just shook his head in disgust and said, "All right, get out of here."

Amber jumped up and ran out of the room slamming the door behind her. She ran out to the back of the school, sat down on the steps, and just fumed as she thought about everything wrong with her life.

CHAPTER 2

Meanwhile, back sitting on the park bench, John Colden thought about what he was going to say and what he was going to do concerning his wife. He got up and slowly headed back towards his house. He walked up the steps, slowly opened the door, and went in. He didn't see Vickie but he heard her rumbling around in the bedroom, so he walked on in. When she saw him she slammed the dresser drawer shut very quickly, like she was hiding something. He looked at her and said, "What you got in there?"

She said, "Nothing that concerns you. It's my own personal stuff, that's all, so it's none of your business."

He didn't say anymore about it. Then he said, "We got to talk."

"What about?" She answered.

John looked around and said, "You know what we've got to talk about, we got to talk about the girls, and we've got to talk about the way we live. This is just no good, I don't like it; I don't like the fighting; I don't like anything that's going on. It's just all got to stop. And I'm telling you something else, too. I don't know what you are up to, I can't put my finger on it, but these secrets between us won't make things better. That said, I have decided I'm going to change my will. The way it is set up right now, in case anything happens to me, you have full conservator ship to take care of the girls. That's just no good."

She looked at him in total shock, as if to say something, except she didn't know what to say. And he said, "Don't say anything. Don't even try to say anything. That's what I'm going to do no matter what you say. It isn't going to make any difference."

She said, "Well you can go to hell, too!" and left the room.

He still had his eyes on the dresser wondering why she slammed it shut so fast. He decided to look. He went over and as he opened the drawer, he saw a needle, cocaine and different kinds of things he knew were drug related, but didn't quite understand what all he was looking at. He really wasn't up on drugs, but he knew what he saw and generally knew what it was used for.

Just then she came back in the room, saw him and yelled, "You get out of there! It's none of your business, that's mine."

"You're a druggie!" John yelled.

"I said get out! It's none of your business, that's mine," she repeated.

He started to take the drugs out of the drawer and she tried to slam the drawer shut, pushing him away. As they struggled, all of a sudden, he felt a tremendous pain in his chest, then grabbed himself where the pain was and let go of her. He stumbled around the room and fell to the floor. She didn't know what happened. She went over to him and knelt down. His eyes were wide open like he was trying to say something and then finally he was very still. Vickie didn't know what to do, she was scared. She ran in the other room and called the police, yelling at them to hurry.

Then she called a doctor and ambulance. Pretty soon there was havoc around the house as the police showed up first, checking him out. Then the ambulance came with the doctor.

After examining him, the doctor looked up at Vickie and said, "I'm sorry, ma'am; I've done all I could. It was too late. He died so fast there was nothing I could do. He was dead before I got here."

Vickie seemed at peace. She said, "That's all right, doctor, you did the best you could. Thank you."

They put John's body in the ambulance and took him to the morgue. When everyone was gone out of the house Vickie just walked around the house now realizing that she was in total control of the house, and for that matter, everything.

She kind of smiled and thought; now I can do what I want to do and nobody can stop me. Things are going to be pretty good for me from now on, she thought. Vickie then got on the phone and called the school to have the girls sent home. She decided to hit things head on right now and get it resolved. She wasn't concerned about John's death as much as she was about letting the girls know who was boss now.

In the meantime at school, Kim was in her English class, standing and reciting a poem for the teacher. Mr. Frazer walked in and asked if Kim could come out into the hallway because he needed to talk to her. Kim put her book down and walked out in the hallway.

Mr. Frazer said, "Kim, I have some real sad news for you about your father."

Kim asked, "Is he sick?"

Mr. Frazer didn't answer.

"Is he real sick?"

Mr. Frazer looked down at the floor. "He is dead," he said. "I'm sorry, Kim." She ran out of the school screaming, heading for home as fast as she could go.

Mr. Frazer finally found Amber sitting out on the back steps of school and told her the same news. Amber began crying and got up and started walking home at a fast pace wondering why all these horrible things were happening to her, why her life was such a mess. Now her father is gone, why is everything happening to her?

Kim walked in the door and saw her step-mother standing in the kitchen waiting for her. Vickie said, "Where's your sister?"

Kim said, "I don't know."

"You don't know?" Vickie yelled. "I sent the word. You both should be here."

About that time Amber came walking in the door and stood beside Kim, they were both crying. Vickie looked at them both and said, "Well, you already got the news this afternoon; your father is dead, so you might as well accept the fact and accept another fact: that I run this house, and what I say goes. I don't want no damn back talk from either of you. You do what I say from now on, and stay out of my room. Stay out of everything. You don't get into anything in my house unless I say you can, and you better not give me any trouble because I know how to take care of it."

Both the girls were pretty numb at the time and really didn't hear much of what she had to say. All they could think about was their father. He was dead and was gone and they didn't know what they were going to do. They just didn't know what they were going to do without their dad.

Vickie had to make all the arrangements for the funeral, but didn't know where to go. There was a little church not more than a block and a half away from their house so she went over to talk to the pastor. She didn't know where else to begin. She was very uncomfortable being in a church. The secretary asked Vickie to be seated and then went to get the pastor.

Jim Harding was a tall man, about 6' 2", and good looking, with a nice smile. He walked up to her and said, "May I help you?"

"Yes," she said, "my husband died and I need some help. I don't know what to do; I've never been through anything like this before."

"Where is your husband's body now?"

"Well, they took it away in an ambulance, to the hospital. I think he's probably at the morgue by now. I don't know for certain where he's at. I'll have to find out."

Pastor Harding said, "All right. I'll help you put it all together. Come in my office and sit down; we'll plan the whole thing out."

He began by asking, "Was your husband a Christian?"

Her reply was, "Hell, I don't know what he was. I don't have any idea."

The Pastor said. "Oh, I see. All right that's a start."

Three days later the funeral was held and John Colden was laid to rest in a cemetery not too far from the little church. As they stood around the casket, before it was lowered in the ground, the Pastor prayed. Then he talked about God and different things that would enlighten the people about death, to help them realize there is GOD and His Love, Jesus Christ and the Holy Spirit and that death is not the end. It's just the beginning. As he talked, the Pastor's wife was also present with their daughter. Standing with Amber, Kim noticed the daughter, Rachel, was in her class. She just never knew Rachel's father was a preacher. She didn't really know Rachel but rather liked her. She seemed to be a nice girl, friendly and easy to be around. These things passed through her mind while she stood and waited for them to lower the casket in the ground.

When it was all over and they started walking away from the grave, Rachel came up to Kim and said, "I'm very sorry for your loss."

"Thank you," Kim said. Rachel then walked with her slowly toward the street to the sidewalk. Rachel said, "Why don't you come over to visit, stay and have dinner with me and my parents sometime? I really don't have very many friends here. I don't associate too much with anybody.

I don't know why, I just never ever got to know anyone that well. Would you think about it?"

Kim said, "Sure." Without saying another word she looked at her and walked off by herself and Rachel went back with her parents.

About two weeks had passed since John had died and the girls had just come back from school one afternoon and as they walked in the house Vickie barked out her orders. "All right, Amber cleans my room and don't you get in any of my drawers. Make my bed and make it look spic and span. Kim, you get in the kitchen and do the dishes, and clean everything up. Scrub the floor, if you ain't got anything else to do."

Kim said, "But I've got homework to do."

Vickie yelled back, "You do your homework after you get the work done in the kitchen. Now get in there and get busy." So both girls went toward their tasks.

Just then the doorbell rang. Vickie answered the door and it was the police. She was startled for a moment because she didn't know what they wanted. The one officer spoke up and said, "Ma'am, does Amber Colden reside here?"

Vickie said, "Yes."

"We'd like to talk to her for a minute."

Vickie hesitated and then said, "Oh, come on in."

They came in and Vickie yelled for Amber to come into the living room. The officer looked at Amber and said, "Are you Amber Colden?"

Amber said, "Yes."

He said, "Have you been hanging around with a fellow named Jake Moran?"

Amber said, "I know him."

"Well, we've seen you with him a few times," he replied, "and wanted to know if you can give us any information about him." Amber said, "I don't know him that well."

"Well, we knew your father, and he was a fine man, and figured maybe you could give us some information. We think Jake is very involved in selling drugs and thought maybe you might be able to help us."

She said, "I don't know anything about drugs. He doesn't do anything like that. He's a good guy."

The officer said, "I see. Then you can't help us?"

Amber said, "No, I can't help you. Goodbye," and turned and went back in the bedroom slamming the door.

The policeman then turned to Vickie and said, "We're sorry we bothered you. I guess we made a mistake. Thank you," and they left. As the two policemen walked towards the car, one of them said, "I think we made a big mistake. I think we really blundered. It will be even harder now."

The other officer agreed, "Yes, we shouldn't have done this, but I had no idea. She's probably his girlfriend and we just didn't know."

As the weeks passed, on the way to school, Amber would duck into the old building near the school. She didn't see Jake. She hadn't seen him for a long time. She didn't know where he could be or what had happened to him. She hadn't gotten any letters, nothing from him, and she was getting anxious.

It had really been a while since she had a fix and didn't know what to do. The withdrawals from the lack of coke were making her really nervous and on edge.

CHAPTER 3

One afternoon as Amber was in her stepmother's bedroom cleaning it and making the bed, she started looking through Vickie's things. She looked on the dresser at different things and she just happened to open the drawer and she saw it. Not only did she see coke, she saw a needle and some other stuff. She really didn't know all the drugs Vickie was on, but she realized then that her stepmother was a drug addict. Now she understood why she Vickie acted the way she did (since Amber also was an addict, only she didn't know it yet). As Amber took a sniff of the coke, her stepmother came into the room and saw her. She reached out and grabbed the bag and then hit Amber hard, knocking her to the floor.

"You little bitch," she said. "I told you not to get into my drawers or anything in my room, didn't I? Didn't I?" She yelled in her face. As she put the stuff back in the drawer she said, "You tell anybody, so help me I'll kill you. Do you hear me? I'll kill you. If I ever see you in my stuff again I'll beat your brains out. You understand me? So now I know, you're hooked on this stuff the same as I am. You got a real problem kid? Well you don't tell, I don't tell. You keep your mouth shut, I'll keep my mouth shut. We understand each other."

Amber stood up and looked at her with a hard glare in her eyes. She said, "I hear you," and she stomped out of the room.

Amber was heading out of the house as Vickie came out of the bedroom. She headed to the kitchen where Kim was doing dishes. She yelled, "Aren't you done yet? You've been in there an hour and you haven't got half of it done. You should be finished. I've got other things for you to do."

Kim said, "I'm doing my best as fast as I can." Vickie hauled off and hit her and she fell to the floor.

As Kim got up she hit her again. "Let that be a lesson to you. When I want something done and I say get it done, you get it done, you hear me?" Then she hauled off and kicked her, walked off into her bedroom and slammed the door yelling back through the closed door, "You better get it done and don't you go nowhere until it's finished."

Kim got up, hurting all over, crying and got busy with the dishes. When she finished, she cleaned up the mess on the floor and ran out the door. She didn't know where she could go. She just had to get out of the house.

As she walked down the street crying, she remembered Rachel asked her to come over to her house. The trouble was, she didn't know where Rachel lived, so she went over to the church and walked in very slowly. She didn't see anybody so she slowly walked down the aisle, looked up and saw a huge cross. Very pretty, she thought. She noticed the church was very beautiful inside. It felt very good as she walked through it. She liked it. Then a lady came out of the office and said, "Can I help you?"

Kim said, "I'm looking for Rachel. She's my friend."

"Oh, Rachel will be at home," the lady said.

"I don't know where she lives," Kim replied. Kim was lying a little bit because she really didn't know Rachel that well. The only time she had talked to her at any length of time was at the funeral for her father.

The lady said, "I'll give you her address," and she gave it to Kim.

Then Kim headed toward Rachel's house. It wasn't very far from the church. Seems like everything is so close, Kim thought. Everything is right around our house. The church is right there and I can run right over to the cemetery and visit my father. Everything is just so close. The school is not very far away either, but this is the worst town and most unhappy place I've ever been.

Living in that town had never been a happy place since her mother died and her father remarried. She was really unhappy as she walked toward Rachel's house. She found the house and rang the doorbell. Rachel's mother, Beverly, answered the door and said, "Well, hello!"

"Hello," Kim returned.

"Aren't you Kim Colden?" Beverly asked.

"Yes," Kim answered. "I came to see Rachel."

Beverly invited her to come in. As she went in, Rachel came out of her room. "Oh! Hi, Kim, I'm glad you came by. Can you stay for supper?"

Kim, who hadn't eaten, all of sudden realized she was hungry. She said, "Well, I guess I could. I can't stay very long though."

Rachel's mother said, "That's fine. We'll set another place at the table, Rachel." Mrs. Harding noticed the marks on Kim's face and she could tell she had been crying. It didn't take much to figure out why.

Rachel hurried to set another place at the table while her mother took care of the food. She was very excited as she tried to keep her poise, for Rachel didn't really have any real close friends at school and she liked Kim, plus she had a deep compassion for Kim losing her father. Rachel felt that a close bond, a kindred spirit, was forming between her and Kim. She wanted this so badly since she was an only child and didn't have any brothers or sisters.

As they sat down, Kim picked up her fork and started to eat when Pastor Harding spoke. "Let's pray."

Looking down, Kim laid her fork down, a little embarrassed. Then Pastor Harding said, "Lord, we thank you for bringing Kim to our home this evening to share our food with us, we feel she is very special in your eyes. Bless the food and we thank you for it, in Jesus' name. Amen." He looked at Kim and with a smile said, "How is your sister doing?"

"I don't know," she said. "She doesn't talk to me much since Dad died. It's like her mind is somewhere else. I don't know why she won't talk to me. I don't know if I've done something wrong. Sometimes I think she's on drugs but I'm sure I'm wrong. I don't think she would do that, although the guy she hangs around with, I've been told is really bad."

"What's his name?" Pastor Harding asked.

"Jake somebody," Kim said. "I don't know his last named, but I've seen Amber sneak into the old building down by the school. That's where she always meets him. Charlie, a black boy at our school, used to hang around with Jake, but he doesn't anymore. I don't know why. I asked him one day and all he said was that he was a bad egg."

Then Kim noticed Rachel, her mother and father were all watching her as she rambled. She suddenly stopped talking and said, "Guess I talk too much, huh?"

"Oh no," said Beverly. "We appreciate the fact you feel free enough and at home, that you would open up your heart to us. Anytime you need to talk to someone you can come here, and we will listen to you. We're good listeners."

Kim smiled and finished eating. Rachel noted to herself that was the first time she had seen Kim smile. After they finished dinner, Kim helped

Rachel clean off the table and helped with the dishes. Then they sat on the floor in front of the TV, talking and giggling in low voices so Rachel's parents couldn't hear what they were talking about.

All of a sudden Kim looked up at the clock and said, "I've got to get home. It's late! Boy, I'm really going to catch it now."

As they walked to the door Kim said goodbye to them. Then as Rachel opened the door she said, "Why don't you come to church Sunday."

Kim thought for a moment and said, "Me? Go to church? You're kidding!"

"No." Rachel said. "Come early to Sunday school. It's just all kids, we have a lot of fun."

"I'll think about it," Kim said as she ran down the steps and down the street.

Running up the steps to her house, she stood for just a minute to catch her breath and think of what she was going to say. She opened the door slowly and walked in. Vickie heard her coming. As she came from the kitchen to the front door with her hands on her hips she said, "Where the hell have you been?"

"Over at a friend's house," Kim said walking slowly toward her room, which she shared with her sister Amber.

Meanwhile, after Kim left Rachel's house, Rachel went to her room. The pastor and his wife were sitting in the living room as he was looking over the new sermons they had sent him from denominational headquarters. He had been reading parts of different sermons when anger started to overcome him and he said to his wife, "Beverly, I can't believe some of the garbage they write in these. They pull scripture out of context to say things that are not true. I mean, I read the Bible," he said, lightly pounding his fist on his desk. "What they're saying just doesn't line up with what is really true. Look here," as he pulled a large drawer open in his desk. "I got sermons written especially to raise money for building projects; for raising money for missions. I've got sermons for every need the church might have and nearly all of them are taken out of context.

Sometimes I feel like a liar when I'm up there preaching."

Beverly got up, walked over to his desk, stood behind his chair and wrapped her arms around his neck. Speaking softly into his ear she said, "Why don't you write your own sermons then?"

The Pastor turned his head around and stared up at her. "You got to be kidding," he said. "The old pillars on the church board would scream blasphemy and have me nailed on a cross if I preached anything they don't want to hear, no matter how true it is."

"Well, it was just a thought," she said as she squeezed him a little.

"It was a good thought," he said looking up at her again. Then he smiled and said, "You're a good kid, if you like kids."

She smiled, then gave him a light slap on the cheek and then kissed him. She went back to the couch and continued reading the book she had. Although she didn't realize it, her husband was thinking seriously about what she had said as he stared out the window.

After a few moments he collected his thoughts and said to her, "It looks like Rachel and Kim are becoming pretty close friends. What do you think about that?"

"What do you mean?" she said.

"Just what I said," he came back with. "What do you think?"

"I think Rachel will be a very good friend and help to Kim," his wife said, kind of puzzled.

"Well," he said, "do you think Kim will be good for Rachel?"

"I think they'll be a great help to each other," she returned.

Pastor Harding said no more as he went back to reading one of his sermons.

Meanwhile, Amber walked up and down the street in front of the theater hoping she just might see Jake. She hadn't heard a thing from him now going on two weeks and that never happened before. Her addiction to cocaine was at its peak and hadn't had a fix since she stole that little bit from her stepmother; she was just about out of her mind. She hung around for a couple of hours, but no Jake. She was getting very desperate. She decided to go over to the old building near the school for one more look before she went home. As she approached the open door to the building, she thought she saw someone's shadow inside. She rushed in without thinking and shouted, "Jake, is that you?"

She heard a voice say "Shhhh," very softly. "Be quiet." She didn't recognize who it was and was a little scared. Then he walked out of the darkness into a little bit of light that was coming through the door. Amber saw that it wasn't Jake.

"Who are you?" she asked.

"A friend of Jake's," he said. "He wanted me to find you and tell you that he would see you soon, and to just hang on."

"What's your name?" Amber asked as he stepped closer.

"People just call me Jimbo," he replied.

Amber could understand why. He was a young man about 18 or 19 years old, about 6 feet 3 inches tall and probably weighed about 250 pounds, easy.

Amber in her desperation asked, "Do you have any coke?"

"Sure," Jimbo replied.

"Can I have some?" she asked, "just a little bit?"

"No," Jimbo said. "That stuff costs money and I ain't rich. If you want some you got to pay."

"But I don't have any money," Amber responded.

"That's just tough," he said as he turned away.

"Please," she begged, "please."

Amber was a very pretty girl and Jimbo was having a hard time resisting her. "Aw, I must be nuts," he said as he handed her a little bit. "That's it. Don't ask for any more unless you get the bucks, understand?"

"Yes, yes. Amber said." After they stood around sniffing coke, Amber said, "Where is Jake?"

"I can't tell," Jimbo said, as he walked toward the door.

Amber grabbed his arm as her anger was aroused! "I want to know where Jake is!" she said in a loud, stern voice

Jimbo looked at her for a moment and replied, "I told you, I can't tell you. Jake would kill me."

"Why, is he in some kind of trouble?" she asked.

"Look, don't ask me any more, I can't tell you."

Then Amber decided she would try to use her charm on him. She got close to him and touched his cheek with her hand and said in a soft voice, "Please Jimbo, tell me where he is, pleeeeease."

That did it. Her soft touch on his fat cheek melted him. He fumbled around with his hands like he didn't know what to do with them and then he said, "Well—well he's in jail. They're trying to pin a rap on him for selling drugs but they won't get away with it. He's too smart. He's smarter than any cop," he laughed.

"Where are they holding him?" Amber asked.

"He's down at the Broadway precinct. They're holding him in the jail there for a few days. I've been in there a couple of times myself," he bragged.

CHAPTER 4

"Thanks, Jimbo," Amber said as she ran out the door, and headed downtown toward the jail. When she arrived in front of the jail, she was a little frightened about going in, but her yearning for Jake overcame her fear as she walked up the steps into the building. Looking around, she noticed a policeman sitting behind his desk, writing. As she stared at him in silence, he finally looked up and saw her.

"What can I do for you?" he said with a large flirtatious grin, as he saw how pretty she was.

Amber slowly walked up to his desk and, stuttering a little asked, "Could I see Jake Moran?"

The officer's smile disappeared from his face when she mentioned Jake's name. "Why would you want to see him?" he said. "A pretty girl like you shouldn't be hanging around a guy like that."

Instantly, Amber's anger overcame her fear. "I didn't ask you for an opinion, thank you! I just want to see Jake, OK!"

"Just a moment," he said. "I'll have to check if it's ok." He got up and went into another room and closed the door behind him. She could hear them talking, but she couldn't understand what they were saying.

Soon the door opened and the officer came out, followed by a man with a suit and tie on. As they walked up to Amber, the officer said, "This is Lieutenant Stearns. He would like to talk to you." Then the policeman went back to his desk.

"What is your name?" the lieutenant asked in a gentle voice.

"Amber," she said.

"And you want to see Jake Moran?"

"Yes," she said.

"What is your relationship with him?" he asked.

"He's my boyfriend," Amber answered.

"I see," said the Lieutenant. "Tell me," he said, as he looked at her face as though he was searching for something, "how long have you known him?"

"A couple of years," Amber said, as she fiddled with her hands.

"All right, I'll let you see him," he said, "but I want to warn you, that boy is headed for real trouble. I hope you have enough sense not to let him drag you down with him."

Amber didn't say a thing, because she didn't want to jeopardize any chance of seeing Jake.

Lt. Stearns led her through two doors, down two hallways, and finally to the cells where the temporary prisoners were held. He told the guard to let her see Jake for a few minutes. The guard opened the cell and let Amber in, as Jake looked up at her totally surprised. When the guard was out of sight, he grabbed her and said, "How did you find me?"

"Jimbo told me."

"I'll kill him," Jake said.

"Don't blame him," Amber said. "I dug it out of him and it wasn't easy."

Jake sat down on his bed saying, "I didn't want you to see me like this. I wish you hadn't come down here." He got up and walked away then sat down again, staring into space.

Amber went over and sat down beside him, reached out and grabbed his hands and held them as she said, "Jake, I love you. I don't care what you've done. I don't know what I'd do without you." She looked away from him.

Jake smiled, pulled her up to him, looked into her eyes and gently reached out and kissed her like he'd never kissed her before. "I love you, too," he said as he kissed her over and over again. "Listen," he said, "I'll be gettin out of here pretty soon. They can't hold me much longer. They ain't got nothing on me."

"Do you have any coke on you?" Amber asked as he held her close.

"Are you kidding? If they found any of that stuff on me, I'd never get out of here. I know how you feel though," he said. "I'm hurting too, and I could sure use some myself."

The guard returned and opened the door. "You have to leave now, Miss," he said.

Amber kissed Jake again and said, "I'll see you soon, honey."

"Yeah," Jake answered, as he watched her intently, "real soon."

As Amber walked out of the police station, her cravings were rapidly getting worse. She needed some cocaine and she needed it bad! As she walked home, she made up her mind to steal some from her stepmother, Vickie. She knew what a chance she would be taking, but at that point she had to have a fix at any cost. She finally reached her home, walked up the steps and quietly entered the house. It was very late, but she didn't turn the lights on as she crept through the house in the dark. She found her way to Vickie's bedroom and quietly slipped in. She could tell Vickie was sleeping heavily by her breathing. She felt her way to the dresser and opened the drawer ever so gently. She felt around and she found what she was looking for. Then she closed the drawer and slipped out of the room. Amber then went into her bedroom she shared with Kim, sat on the edge of the bed and began sniffing the coke when the light went on. It was Kim who had woke up, slipped out of bed and turned on the light to see what was going on.

"Turn out that light." Amber whispered harshly.

Kim walked up to Amber, staring at her as if she never heard her and said, "What are you doing?"

"Just sniffing coke," Amber said.

"Not you," Kim said as she stood watching her.

"Why not?" Amber returned. "It won't hurt you."

"Why do you do it?" Kim asked.

"Because it makes me feel good," Amber answered. "It picks you up when you're down, gets you going again."

"It destroys your brain in the process," Kim said.

"Don't believe everything you hear," Amber said. "there's no truth in that stuff."

"That's what you think," Kim returned. "I can show you some kids at school who've been on that stuff a long time and they've turned into morons. They lie, cheat, steal and stink 'cause they don't have any dignity or even enough self respect to take a bath."

"Just shut up!" Amber said. "You don't know what you're talking about."

"Yes I do," Kim answered.

About that time the door flew open and Vickie entered the room. Amber was caught red handed.

"What's going on in here?" Vickie asked as she walked up to Amber sitting on the bed. Vickie saw what Amber had. She swung and hit Amber in the head and knocked her off the bed. Vickie bent down, picked up the coke, and with her face almost touching Amber's face as Amber sat up, she said, "I told you never to get in my stuff, didn't I? I told you what I'd do to you, didn't I?" as she hit her again. "I'm warning you for the last time. I'll break your neck if you get in my stuff again." Vickie stormed out of the room slamming the door behind her.

Kim helped Amber up and on the bed. "She really scares me," Kim said, shaken by the whole episode. Amber got up, walked into the bathroom, washed her face, put on her nightgown and went to bed, thinking of all the things she'd like to do to Vickie, until she fell asleep.

It was late morning the next day, after Kim and Amber had long gone to school, when the phone rang. Vickie, still in bed, reached over and grabbed it. "Hello," she said, still half asleep.

"Mrs. Colden," the voice said at the other end of the phone.

"Yeah," she said.

"This is Mr. Jenkins. I'm an attorney and was a close friend of your late husband, John, and I also have his will on file here. I thought now would be a good time to have the reading. It requires that you and both his daughters be present."

Vickie sat up in bed quickly since she didn't know much about John's will. She had forgotten all about it. She arranged for the appointment to be on Saturday morning rather than on a school day.

Saturday morning came quickly as Vickie, Amber & Kim walked into Mr. Jenkins office. He greeted them all and had them sit at a table. He gathered all his papers together and sat down with them. "Well," he said with a smile, "I guess we might as well get started. I'll read John's will first, then, when I am finished, I will interpret or answer your questions, OK?"

They all acknowledged OK.

I John declare that my wife, Vickie, be in complete charge of all property and money until each one of the girls, Amber and Kimberly, reach the age of twenty-one. The property includes the home and the monies that come from both my insurance policies. Each will receive one third of all properties and money. When Kim, the youngest reaches age Twenty-one, then all three can vote on what to do with the property by majority rule.

Signed by John Colden."

Vickie, doing everything she could do to act like a sweet and sad wife, said, "We really don't know how much insurance John had. I haven't yet taken the time to look through all his papers."

Well," Mr. Jenkins said, "he had two life insurance policies on himself: one for one hundred-fifty thousand, and one for one hundred thousand dollars. He also had another that will pay the girls two thousand dollars a month until age twenty-one."

Vickie's eyes bugged out of her head and it took everything she had to keep her composure. She had no idea he had that kind of insurance.

"Now," Mr. Jenkins continued, "Vickie will have control of the two thousand dollars a month income per child until the girls - you, Amber and you, Kimberly - until you reach 21 years of age."

"That's not fair," Amber yelled, jumping up from her chair. "She'll spend it all. Kim and I will never see a penny of that money. You wait and see."

"Why Amber," Vickie said, as calm and sweet as she could be, "how can you, say that? I've always tried to be a good mother." She glanced towards Mr. Jenkins with a nervous smile.

"A good mother!" both girls screamed.

"You're a witch!" Amber yelled. "A wicked old witch!"

Vickie took a handkerchief out of her purse and pretended to cry like her feelings were hurt. Mr. Jenkins could see how phony it was. As he got up from the table he said, "I would like to speak to Amber and Kim alone, Mrs. Colden, if you would wait out in the reception room, please. Thank you," he said before Vickie had a chance to object.

He asked the girls to sit down again. Kim was crying and Amber had a hard, angry, stony look on her face. "Girls," he said, with sadness in his voice, "your father had called me the day before he died and told me that he was going to change his will because of the conditions in your home with your stepmother. But unfortunately, he didn't get down and get it done. It's a shame he didn't get the chance. But I will file a petition with the court and see if it's possible to get a Judge to overrule the will. It might take a long time, a year, maybe two, I don't know. I'll do the best I can. I liked your father very much and don't want to see his kids be taken advantage of," he said in anger. "Until then, I can't do anything. If you have any real problems and you need to talk to someone for any reason, please call me. It's free," he said, trying to lighten the mood.

Then he led them out of his office where Vickie was and bid them goodbye and winked at the girls. Vickie saw the wink as the girls smiled at him. It worried her, for she didn't know what it was about. As they walked out of the building, Vickie couldn't hold it back any longer as she lashed out. "Ok girls, let's get one thing straight. I still run the show so you'd better not give me any crap, you hear? I don't care what kind of deal you got with that damn attorney. I hold the reigns, you understand?" Amber and Kim just glared at her without giving her an answer.

CHAPTER 5

Monday morning rolled around and Amber and Kim were off to school. Kim went at a fast walk while Amber just poked along. They seldom ever walked to school together. As Amber passed the old building near the school, she heard someone call out to her. She had a broad smile as she rushed into the building because she knew by his voice exactly who it was. It was Jake. She rushed into his arms, hugging and kissing him, and telling him how much she missed and loved him. Amber told Jake about her father's will and how Vickie had control of everything. "Boy, is she a witch," Jake said, shaking his head. "Someday she'll get hers. What goes around comes around. Ya just watch and see."

Jake pulled some coke out of his pocket and they both indulged. Then Jake told Amber the bad news. "I'm just out on bail," he said. "I go to trial, who knows when, maybe three or four months away. The courts are so crowded it might even be longer."

"You mean you're not free?" Amber said.

"No," he answered, "but don't worry, they ain't gonna pin nothin on me. I'm not gonna worry bout it," he said as he gave her some coke to take with her.

"Oh wow," Amber said, "I'm late for school again, I got to run; I just might make it." She dashed out the door, stopped, rushed back in, kissed Jake and then ran out the door and disappeared onto the school grounds. She quickly hit her locker, grabbed her books and then paused, reaching in her pocket, taking out the coke and stashed it in her locker. Then she ran to class.

Lunch time rolled around and Kim and Rachel were carrying their trays through the cafeteria looking for a table. They finally found one, sat down, and began eating, talking and giggling when suddenly a boy sat down at their table and said, "Hi, do you mind if I join you? I couldn't find any place to sit."

Kim and Rachel just looked at each other kind of puzzled since there were plenty of empty tables around the cafeteria. They both recognized the boy. He was Jeff Miller, a very good looking and popular boy at school. He was a junior, one year ahead of Kim and Rachel and they were surprised he would associate with them being as they were underclassmen.

As they began eating again he looked at Kim and said, "You're Kim, right? And I don't know your name," as he looked at Rachel.

"I'm Rachel," she said with a slight smile.

Then his eyes went back to Kim and he stared at her face a few seconds as he ate. He made a gesture with his hand and said, "You know, a bunch of guys were talking and decided that you are probably one of the prettiest girls in school."

"Oh, really?" Kim said as she looked at Rachel and winked. "What are you after?"

"Nothing," he said, kind of puzzled. "I was just stating a fact." He was quiet for a minute and then looked at Kim, again making a funny gesture with his hand and said, "Would you like to go to the movies with me, maybe Friday or Saturday night?"

"You're asking me for a date?" Kim asked.

"Well, yeah," he said with a smile.

"I'll think about it," Kim said, sipping on her drink.

"What?" he returned. "What's there to think about? It's yes or no, right?"

"I'll think about it," Kim repeated.

"Ok, ok," Jeff said as he got up, picked up his tray and moved on.

"How could you do that?" Rachel said as he disappeared. "Every girl in school would give their right arm to go out with him."

"I'm not every girl in school," Kim returned. "Besides, I'm not that impressed with him. Sure he's cute, but there's got to be more than that to a person. He's probably so in love with himself there isn't room for anyone else."

"Well, I hope you know what you're doing," Rachel said. "I think he's gorgeous."

"Well maybe we can fix him up with you," Kim kidded.

"Are you kidding?" Rachel replied. "I don't look like you." Kim just smiled as they got up and dropped off their trays and headed back towards the school grounds.

It was Sunday morning. Kim's alarm sounded and she quickly turned it off before it woke Vickie up. She decided to go to Sunday school, anything, to get out of the house. After all, it couldn't be that bad. She showered, got dressed, ate, brushed her teeth and was on her way. As she entered the church, looking around, she didn't know where to go. Then Mrs. Harding came out of one of the rooms, saw Kim, and walked up to her with a big smile.

"Kim, I'm so glad you came. Rachel will be so happy. Come on, I'll take you to her."

They went through a door which took them into another building attached to the church. As they walked down the hallway, Kim noticed by the writing on the doors that the kids were divided by their age into different groups. Hmm, just like school, she thought. She had no idea what she was in for since she had never been to Sunday school or Church in her life. Then they stopped at another door, Mrs. Harding opened it and in they went. Rachel was sitting in a chair close to the front, an empty place next to her. Kim hurried and sat down beside her.

"I saved the seat for you, hoping you'd show up," Rachel said.

Kim had a look of shock on her face as she looked around the room. There were at least sixty or seventy kids she recognized from school. As she glanced around some smiled and some waved to her. She had no idea so many kids went to church. You would never know it when you see them in school, for they just look like everybody else. They don't act weird or anything, so how can you tell, she thought.

Then Mrs. Cambell came into the room. As she walked up in front of the class, she noticed Kim and said, "We have a visitor in our class today and your name is...?"

"Kim," Rachel spoke up. "She's my best friend."

"Well," Mrs. Cambell continued, "Pastor Harding has agreed that since we have so many high school students, we need a high school choir."

"Oh, no," some of the boys groaned.

"Now pay attention," she said loudly, to make sure she had been heard. We'll have individual tryouts starting with a girl first and then a boy. This is not to see how good you can sing, but to find out what level of voice range you have, for instance a tenor or a baritone."

"OK," Mrs. Cambell said again, as she sat down at the piano. "I want all the girls to sit on the left side of the room and all the boys on the right."

As the kids moved around to their new seats, she played a song called. "In the Garden". When they all finished moving and settled down, she stopped and said, "All right, you know this song, so this is what we'll sing." She then had a girl in the front row sing, and then a boy after each girl.

As they went through the rotation, it finally came to Rachel and then a boy. Then it was Kim's turn. She was very scared; she never did anything like this in front of an audience before. As the teacher watched her smiling, Kim just sat there.

"Would you like to try?" Mrs. Cambell asked.

"I can't sing," Kim returned.

"Who cares?" she said. "God doesn't judge us by how good we can sing. He just wants us to try." Kim got up slowly and walked to the piano, very nervous. She cleared her throat as she waited for Mrs. Cambell to start playing. Since Kim had already heard the song about 20 times, she had it memorized. She was still very nervous as she started singing. But after a couple of verses, she calmed down and was enjoying it and her voice got stronger and louder. As she came near to the end of the song, she noticed Rachel, all the kids, and Mrs. Cambell were staring at her like she'd never seen anyone look at her before. As she ended, it was so quiet you could hear a pin drop. Then all the kids broke out clapping and cheering. When they settled down, Mrs. Cambell said with a very sober face, "We've never had anyone who could sing like that, so please forgive us for our behavior. Have you had voice training?"

"No," Kim said, "I've never sang before."

"You have a beautiful voice," Mrs. Cambell said. "You're just wonderful." She jumped up from the piano and gave her a big hug. Then she went back to the piano and called for the next person to sing.

Kim returned to her seat and while she sat, Rachel was still staring at her with her mouth wide open. Then she whispered in Kim's ear, "Wow, you are so good. I wish I could sing like you."

When Sunday school was over and the kids headed for the main sanctuary for regular service, many came by Kim to congratulate her on how well she sang. Kim was stunned. She had no idea she could sing. Then she got a little lost in thought, back in time, remembering her father telling her what a wonderful singer her mother was. She must have gotten her voice from her mother.

CHAPTER 6

In church, as they started to sit down, everyone else stood up and began singing *How Great Thou Art*, a beautiful song Kim had never heard before. Pastor Harding walked up to the pulpit. As he put his Bible and notes down, he looked out over the congregation. "Before I start my sermon this morning, I'd like to talk about something that's been bothering me for a while. I've been reading in the papers about all the drug problems with the young people in our town. They blame organized gangs and peer pressure from friends as well as enemies. I agree with that only a little. Very little! I firmly believe, because of what the Bible teaches about our children, especially in Proverbs. I believe the crucial learning time for our children, the time for us parents to be a great influence on them, is between the ages of one and twelve. I've heard parents say that children raise themselves and that we parents just supply a place for them to sleep and eat. Some parents feel the teachers should raise them. A teacher once said to me that teacher's are just glorified baby-sitters. My answer to that is 'Hogwash. It's just a cop-out for not wanting to take responsibility for raising our children. You want to get crime off the streets by laying it all on the police, but if we did our part in their young lives, the police wouldn't have such a tough job like they have now. Children are no different than adults as far as their feelings are concerned, especially when they're very young." He paused as he walked back and forth. "They want to be noticed, they want attention, they want someone to tell their troubles to, someone to communicate with, and most of all they need you to love them above everything else. At this age level, they need to be taught right from wrong, to be disciplined. They want to be disciplined," he said loudly.

"And you know something else!" he said as he looked over the congregation. "If you show how much you care and love them, they'll love you back. In a day and age where, in many cases, both parents are working, or are just too busy to pay attention to their children, they soon reach junior high and suddenly you have problems with them you never bargained for. You get angry with them because they're not what you want them to be. You see, they did raise themselves. You weren't around to give them any input, so don't blame them; you did in fact get exactly what you asked for. Now you want them to change, to be good, but it's a little late. So as they get in to high school, it's easier to blame the teachers than to look at yourself, right! It's been said most of the teen-agers involved in crime come from broken homes. That's only partly true. At least they have an excuse. What's ours? Some folks like to say most of the crime comes from the African-American and Mexican community. Why? Because they're black or brown? Or is it, maybe because they're under privileged? We live in our nice homes with nice cars with our good jobs. They live on the other side of town, in homes run down and falling apart that you and I wouldn't let our dog live in. How come they live like this? They steal or do what ever they have to survive.

"Some of you older adults, think back before and after the depression of the 20's and 30's when you and your families lived in shacks, working fourteen hours a day seven days a week for next to nothing for wages, stealing food or whatever you could so that you and your family could survive. It's not much different today, is it, for our minorities, all because of the color of their skin. That's sad and it's wrong. How many African-Americans or Mexicans do we have in our congregation?" he said, looking around. "I haven't seen any since I've been your pastor, which has been a little over a year."

He was quiet for a moment, walking back and forth very slowly, his eyes quickly glancing around the congregation again, watching their faces. On some he saw anger, some he saw compassion, some tears, but mostly he saw faces with blank looks of shock at what he was saying. He decided there was no turning back from his thoughts now, but to see it through. So he continued, "These kids come from all kinds of homes. Rich homes with parents who buy them anything they want, homes where both parents work, and homes with families so poor they can hardly survive. The end result: street kids, thousands of them, looking for what they're missing in their home, love, in their lives. And they'll get it anyway they can," he said, leaning toward the congregation. "A small percentage of them will choose hard crime to suffice their needs. Nearly all of them will turn to drugs. Some of them will wake up, see what they're becoming and make the choice to make something decent out of their lives. But the bulk of them will walk in *CONFUSION!* They will not know where to turn or what to do since the hurt is so deep. Some of them commit suicide because they feel they can't handle it anymore," he said loudly, almost shouting. "Parents walk in confusion because they don't know what's wrong with their kids. After all, they did everything they could for them. They brought them into the world. If it weren't for them, they wouldn't even be alive. They look for excuses and answers from psychologists, to teachers, to friends, but never looking to what the problem really is, because if they do, they have to change their life style. They would have to give a little time to their children. Thank God there are a lot of parents who realize and understand. But do you know what the greatest thing missing in these children's lives is? It is the Spirit of God. God," he shouted, "through Jesus Christ can give them Love, Compassion and Guidance. God, who is able to show them how important they are to Him. What kind of programs do we have to help those on the streets? None," he stated. "Are we even looking into doing something in that direction? If not, then we should."

He walked to the podium, opened his Bible, looking up over the congregation and closed his Bible again. He stepped away from the podium again as he said, "Let me instill this in your minds. Columbus was a God fearing man and even though he didn't know he discovered a new country, God did, and that's all that counts. He saw that it was recorded. The pilgrims were the first Christians to settle in America, establish freedom of religion, which spread throughout the 13 colonies. The group of men who wrote our constitution, were all Christians except for one man. The constitution written was based on Christian principles—free men in charge of their own destiny instead of by a King or a dictator. Our first President George Washington was a God fearing Christian and had he not been we might live under a dictatorship today. We wouldn't be the prosperous nation that we are. God blessed our nation with a Christian President during the civil war. He knew the nation had to stand undivided, united as one, if it were to survive. Through all that, two hundred years later, we have made amendments and passed laws making it so Christ can not be taught or even talked about in our schools despite the fact Christian's formed the first schools in our country. We can't even talk about Christ on the school grounds. Whose fault is that? It's our fault, us the so-called Christians.

We're so busy fighting among ourselves between all our different denominations and built the walls up so high between us that we've gotten away from the things of God. I'll tell you something else, those walls will have to come down before we are able to solve all the problems we have with our walk with God. We have to learn to quit judging each other. That's God's job. I'm not saying all the churches should disappear and there be only one church. I'm simply saying, we all have to get along and work together to do God's work in accordance with his will, his plan. We have to learn to love each before we can love anyone else. When we learn that, we can become a powerful tool for God in this world."

Then he slowly walked back to the podium and as he opened his Bible, he said, "Some of what I've just told you is factual and some is strictly my opinion, so I don't want you to leave hear thinking everything I said is Gospel. Thank you. And now let's begin our service," he said as he opened his notebook and Bible and began preaching their usual order of service.

CHAPTER 7

When church was over and Pastor Harding went to the door to say goodbye as people left, Kim and Rachel just hung around until most people had left. As they sat, they heard people remarking on the sermon and saying things like "what nerve, how dare he say those things to us about our children; or who does he think he is anyway; or I think he's right on. One thing for sure, the Elders of the church were quite upset with his forward to the sermon. At the end of the line folks headed out, Elder Joe Clark, head of the Elder board, asked Pastor Harding to come to a special meeting after everyone had left. The pastor nodded yes.

The last person in the line was a short, husky-built man with a friendly look on his face. He came up to shake hands and said, "My name is John Costa and I'm an Elder at a church in Green River, about 150 miles from here. I was visiting friends this week and just thought I'd visit another church this morning. I was most impressed with your opening statement before service. You seem to have your heart in the right place. I hope to hear you again sometime."

"Thank you," said Pastor Harding. "I really appreciate that."

Then the Pastor told his wife, Beverly, to take the girls and head home so he could attend the special meeting called by the Elders. She looked concerned as she walked out of the church with Kim and Rachel.

Pastor Harding entered his office where the Elders were waiting for him. He could tell by the look on their faces it wasn't going to be pleasant. As he closed the door, Elder Clark jumped at him like a vulture. "How dare you tell the people what's wrong with the kids in our town! As if it's their fault! Your job is just to preach sermons. That's what you get paid for, nothing else. It's not our problem what goes on in the streets. The police should take care of that. Do you hear me?"

Pastor Harding's temper was rising and he was doing everything he could to keep it under control. Then he spoke quietly as he gritted his teeth, "It is our problem... what's going on in the streets. It's our responsibility to reach out in our community. God gave us that responsibility when it comes to our children. I'm trying to wake our church up to the fact we have a mission field right in our own backyard, same as in any foreign country, and it's our job to help save our own kids just as well as other countries."

"That's not your job," Elder Clark yelled. "We run this church. You just work here, do you understand?"

At that point Pastor Harding lost his cool. He leaped forward bent down and got his face right in Elder Clark's face and yelled, "Now you listen to me! It's the job of everyone when the children are concerned; mine, yours, the people in the church and the kid's parents. How can you possibly say that it's not my job? If it's not, and you run the church, then why aren't you doing something about it instead of standing here yelling at me, huh?"

Elder Clark was startled and shocked by the anger and forcefulness that came from the Pastor. He immediately backed down. He'd never seen him like this before and it scared him a little. He looked at the other Elders and motioned to them to leave as he backed out the door himself. "Well, we'll see about that," he said as he darted out the door.

Pastor Harding took his robe off and put on his coat. He was very upset with himself for allowing his temper to get the best of him.

When he reached home and walked in the door, Beverly could tell he was upset. "What happened?" she asked, helping him with his coat.

"I really did it," he said quietly. "I really did it. I let old man Clark gets the best of me and I lost my head. I really let him have it. I was all over him like a fly on molasses. Why did I allow him do that to me? I have no excuse. I just need to have more self control in those situations," he said as he ran his hand over his face and through his hair.

Then he turned to his wife again and asked where the girls were. "They're in Rachel's room," she said. Then she added, to change the subject, "You should have heard what Mrs. Cambell said about Kim. Apparently, she has one of the most beautiful voices she ever heard. She thinks with some coaching, she can be a wonderful singer. She can hardly wait to get the High School choir started practicing. She's on cloud nine right now."

"Good," Pastor Harding replied. "Kim needs something positive in her life right now."

He looked at Beverly, smiled and said, "I think I'll go lie down and take a nap," as he started to the bedroom.

"Aren't you hungry?" she asked.

"No, not right now," he said, as he went through the door and closed it.

Kim and Rachel sat looking out the window as they talked. Then Kim, looking very serious, asked

Rachel, "Do I really sing well or do you think they were just trying to make me feel good?"

"Kim! I'm telling you, you were fantastic," Rachel pleaded. "I just wish you could have heard yourself." Then Rachel changed the subject by asking, "Are you going to go out with Jeff?"

"I probably will," Kim returned, "but I'll wait a while before I tell him. He's so full of himself it will be good for him to have to wait. I don't want to make his ego any bigger than it already is." Rachel just looked at Kim and shook her head in wonder. Kim smiled at her.

"Well, I better get home," Kim said. "I hate to go back to my house. You don't even know what its like," she said as she stared out the window. Then she gathered up her things and Rachel walked her to the door.

Kim entered her home and the first thing she noticed was that Vickie wasn't there. As she went to her room, Amber was sitting on the bed sniffing coke. Kim yelled, "Amber! Are you crazy? You know what she said she'd do to you if she caught you in her stuff again."

"What is the matter with you? I didn't get it from her," Amber replied.

"Where did you get it then?" Kim asked.

"None of your business." Amber replied,

"I'll bet you got it from Jake," Kim said.

"You don't know what you're talking about. Just shut up!" Amber yelled. "You hear me, just shut up!"

Kim went over, sat on her bed and just watched Amber. After a moment she spoke up again and said, "Amber, you are so stupid."

Amber hauled off and hit Kim across the face, knocking her off the bed to the floor. Kim put her arm across her face to protect herself. She started crying as she looked at Amber with fear in her eyes. Amber suddenly realized what she had done. She got down with Kim, grabbed her and hugged her, begging her to forgive her. "I'm so sorry Kim," she said, as she started crying also. "I didn't mean it, honey. I'm sorry, I'm so sorry." She rocked her as she held her in her arms. "I'm so mixed up, I have so many problems and I don't know what I'm doing sometimes. I didn't mean it, honey. Will you forgive me?"

Kim nodded her head yes and smiled through her tears. They got up from the floor and sat on the bed. Kim asked as she reached out and held Amber's hand, "What's happening to you, Amber? You are changing so much. Sometimes I feel like I don't even know you anymore."

"I don't know," Amber said. "I'm so confused. I don't know why we have to be punished just because Dad died. We have to live here with that bitch." As more tears came to her eyes, Amber continued, "Sometimes I get so angry at Daddy for dying and leaving us here with her. It's just not fair; it's just not fair." Her voice drifted off.

"But Daddy isn't here," Kim said. "You're all I have and I'm all you have. Can't we try to get along and help each other the best we can?"

Amber looked at Kim through her tears, grabbed her, hugged her and said, "Sure we can. I don't know what I'd do without my baby sister."

About that time they heard someone come into the house. There was more than one person and they knew that one of the voices belonged to Vickie. Suddenly the door swung open to their bedroom and Vickie walked in. "Well, you both are here," she said in a surprised voice. Then a man stepped into the room beside Vickie. Amber and Kim had never seen him before. "This is Paul," Vickie said, then she and Paul went out the door and closed it.

"Do you think he's her new boyfriend?" Kim asked.

"I don't know," Amber said, "but he better not try to move in here. This is our home. He's got no business here."

Kim continued, "You know, I saw Vickie talking to a guy down on the corner, one night before Dad died, but I couldn't see what he looked like."

Vickie and Paul went into the kitchen. Paul sat down at the table and Vickie poured him a glass of whiskey. Paul was a big man, about 6 ft tall, around 200 lbs, with a ruddy complexion, about average looking. He had dark eyes that always seemed to be looking through you.

Amber came out of her room, went in the kitchen and got a glass of water just as an excuse to get a better look at him. As she walked back past him towards her room, she looked back at him. He smiled at her as he undressed her with his eyes. Vickie saw his face as Amber disappeared into her room. "Just keep your hands off her. Any thing you need, I can give you," she said with a sly smile.

"She's a cute kid," he said as he sipped on his drink. "Very cute," he repeated as he stared at Amber's door.

Amber took her glass of water and set it down on the table near her bed. She looked over at Kim and said, "Ugh, he makes my skin crawl." She shrugged as if she had a chill. "I didn't like the way he looked at me," she mumbled as she got up and walked to the window.

CHAPTER 8

Meanwhile Vickie poured herself a drink, walked over and sat down at the table across from Paul. She stared at him for a moment and then said, "I'm your girl, Paul, and don't you forget it. I saw the way you looked at her. If you ever mess around with another girl I'll claw your eyes out, do you hear me?"

He smiled and took another sip of his drink. "You don't own me," he said. "We're just business partners remember." He got up from the table.

"You know," he said as he looked back at Vickie, "I've been thinking about another line of business to add to our venture in the drug business."

Vickie spoke out, "Like what?"

He walked over to the sink and poured himself another drink, took a sip and said, "Well, I've been thinking about prostitution. You know if it's run right, it could be a profitable business. Yes," he said with more sureness in his voice, "with some more girls pretty as the one you got in there." He pointed towards Amber's room.

"You're talking about a prostitution ring?" Vickie asked as she watched him, his mind preoccupied with making plans. She broke his train of thought when she said, "I don't know if she's ever been touched." She watched him pacing up and down.

"Well, we will just have to teach her all about life."

"I guess you'll be the one to teach her, huh," she responded in disgust.

"Why not," he said with a smile. "She's got to learn from somebody the finer things in life." Then he laughed. "I'll check with some of our pushers. They ought to be able to give me a line on some cute kids who are addicts and need the money."

"I don't know about Amber," Vickie replied. "She's a pretty stubborn kid."

"She's an addict, right?" Paul said. "You cut her off and she'll come around."

"I don't know, she's pretty stubborn," Vickie repeated.

Paul was staring at Amber's bedroom door and spoke without looking back. "We'll see, heh, heh, we'll see. In fact, the more I think about it, the more I like it. I think I'll start working on it right now." He went out the door so preoccupied that he didn't even say anything to Vickie as he left.

Vickie just sat with mixed emotions. She loved Paul very much, but she didn't let it show too much because of her pride; she knew he couldn't be trusted with women. She saw he was developing a keen eye for Amber and her jealousy and hatred towards Amber grew even more as she sat trying to figure how she could stop him from putting his hands on Amber the first chance he got.

Paul was her business partner for selling cocaine and a very good one. She had teamed up with him way back before she married John Colden, and he had steadily made their drug business grow. He controlled the pushers on the street, and they feared him, because he was so mean and had no conscience. She felt like she was caught between a rock and a hard spot. One thing she knew for sure, she didn't want to do anything to upset the apple cart, so for now, she would do nothing.

Amber was looking out the window when she saw Paul leave the house, go down the street, jump into his car and drive off. She turned and walked to her door, not saying anything to Kim, opened it and went into the kitchen where Vickie was sitting at the table sipping on a drink. "Who's he?" she asked.

"Just a friend," Vickie said, staring off into space.

"Have you known him a long time?" Amber asked, walking around the room in a slow zig zag pattern, with her hands behind her, never looking up from the floor.

"That's none of your damn business," Vickie retorted angrily.

"Just curious," Amber said, as she retreated back to her room, closing the door behind her.

She walked over and sat down on her bed, looked over at Kim and said, "There is definitely something fishy about that guy. I think I've seen him before, I know I have."

Morning came quickly and Amber and Kim were off to school. Only a few more weeks and school would be out for the summer. Kim rushed around the corner where she always met Rachel, and Amber headed for the old building near the school to meet Jake, if he showed up.

Rachel and Kim were walking along towards school when Kim said, "Vickie brought a strange guy home with her yesterday, or at least he was strange to me. He scares me. I mean the way he looks at me makes my skin crawl. I sure hope he doesn't start coming around a lot. I couldn't stand to be around him."

"Well," laughed Rachel, "you can spend more time over at my house. My parents really like you.

I don't have brothers or sisters, so you can sort of be my sister. I've always wanted one. It's no fun being alone." Ha! Ha!" Kim replied, "it's better then the way I'm living now."'

"There's choir practice tonight at the church, don't forget," Rachel said, as they rounded the corner to the school.

Meanwhile, Amber reached the old building and went in looking for Jake. She called out in a loud whisper, "Jake, where are you? Are you here?" She listened for a few seconds and then called again, but no answer. She walked out of the building a little depressed and headed for school.

Rachel and Kim were getting their books out of their lockers when they turned, and there was Jeff looking at them with a smile. He said to Kim, "There's a new movie coming out Friday night; would you like to go with me?"

Kim looked at him for a second and said, "I'll have to ask my..." Then she stopped, realizing she almost said 'mother', which is something she would never call Vickie. "I'll have to ask permission. That's if I decide to go. I'll let you know before Friday, ok?" she said, as she and Rachel rushed off to class.

As they got to their class and sat down, Rachel said, "Are you going to go out with him?"

Kim didn't answer.

"Tell me before I go crazy."

Kim smiled and said, "I think so, if I can get away from Vickie. That will be the biggest problem. I never know what she's going to say." Then the teacher started calling attendance.

After school, Amber headed back to the old building looking for Jake. As she entered she heard someone talking. She followed the sound of the voices until she saw Jake talking to two young boys. Approaching, she heard someone running towards her from the direction she came into the building. She quickly hid behind a half torn down wall. She saw Jake handing the boys something that she figured was coke as two men rushed past her. Jake took off running toward a door in the back of the building, but they caught him before he could get out. She saw one of the men take out a pair of handcuffs from his pocket and slap them on Jake's wrists. One man then took Jake out the front of the building while the other man brought out the two boys. As they disappeared out of the building, Amber slipped quietly to the front opening and watched through a crack in a wood covered window and listened to what they were saying.

"We've got you this time, scum. You won't get out of this one. You're going to get nailed this time and get what you deserve." They read him his rights and put him in the back seat of a police car and drove off. They put the two young boys in the back seat of another police car and took them also. Amber was scared. She wondered just how much trouble Jake was in. How was she going to know what was happening to Jake?

When it looked safe, she darted out of the door and ran home.

Meanwhile. Kim called Vickie from school and asked if she could go straight over to Rachel's for the rest of the evening. Vickie told her yes, since she didn't like the girls around unless there was work to do.

When school was over, the two girls headed for Rachel's house and went in. "Hi, Mom," Rachel said, kissing her on the cheek. Then they went into Rachel's room and got busy doing their homework, and getting ready for final exams, only a week away. Afterward, they had supper and went back to Rachel's room and sat talking for a while, then decided to practice some of the songs they would be singing in the choir. Rachel went to the piano and they began singing.

Pastor Harding and Beverly sat on the couch and talked about the events for the coming week. Jim looked at his wife and said, "I'm writing another sermon, but I don't know if I'll preach it on Sunday. I have a lot of things I'd like to say about our love towards God." He chuckled as he said, "After I preach a sermon like that maybe they'll ride me out of town on a rail."

"Do you really think the congregation would act like that?" Beverly said, kind of puzzled.

"No, not the congregation," he responded, "but the Elders and Deacons — well that's another story. They're still pretty hot over the last one I wrote. But, I really feel I've got to teach the truth of the Gospel or I have no business wearing this cloth," he said.

They talked a while about other programs for the week and then, as they were getting up to go about other personal business around the house, the girls came out of Rachel's room. "We're going over to the church to choir practice," Rachel said, as they headed for the door.

"Have fun," her mother hollered after them as they left.

When they arrived, most of the kids were already present. Mrs. Cambell was unlocking the door when she looked up and saw Pastor Harding walking towards the church. Then he turned and headed for his office. Mrs. Cambell said to the kids, "Look over your music and study the words until I return." She headed over to the Pastor's office, and knocked.

"Come in," he said as he sat at his desk looking over some papers.

"Pastor, I have a terrible problem within myself over the music I'm preparing for the High School choir."

"What's the problem; it can't be that serious."

"Well," she said, fumbling with the sheet of paper she had in her hand, "the music I want to use isn't in our hymnal book, which is approved by denominational headquarters. I just love this music I have. These songs were written in the last few years and are relatively new, but they're so good."

"Let me see them," Pastor Harding said, getting up from his chair. She walked up and handed them to him. He looked them over for a minute and handed them back to her, turned and walked back to his desk without saying a word. Then suddenly he turned and looked at her, smiled and said, "Go ahead and use them. I'm sure it will be fine."

"Oh, thank you," she said, and she hurried out the door and back to the practice room where the kids were waiting. As she walked into the room, the kids could tell by the expression on her face that she was happy about something.

"All right, up on the stage, and take your places," she said as she sat down at the piano and placed her music in front of her. "Ok, we'll start on page one, a new song. Well, for us a new song. It's called *Turn Your Radio On*." As Mrs. Cambell started playing, the kids knew they were going to like this fast, modern song. They went over it several times trying to learn the words and music properly and get it all down pat.

All of a sudden she stopped, thought for a moment and said, "I think it would be better if we had a lead soloist with the choir backing it up." She looked directly at Kim as she spoke. Kim was struck with fear; she knew what was coming.

"Kim, I believe we'll try you first."

Kim stood frozen in her tracks. Then she said, "If I sing, does it mean I will have to stand up in front of all the people in the church and do it, too?"

"Yes," Mrs. Cambell said softly, for she saw how scared Kim was.

"No Way," Kim said. "I could never do that in a million years."

"You can do it, Kim," then the rest of the kids started saying "Kim, Kim, Kim." They kept chanting.

"All right, all right, that's enough," Mrs. Cambell said as she walked up to Kim. She took her by the hand and led her away from the choir over to another part of the room to talk privately. "There are lots of things in life we must conquer. In your life, this is one of them. Right now you're a little scared. We'll practice and practice until we know it backwards and forward and until you get enough confidence, then if you still don't think you can do it, we'll just sing it as a choir without a soloist."

"Well, ok," Kim said, "I'll try under those conditions." They went back up on the stage and everyone took their places and began again, but this time Kim sang the lead and the choir backed her up. Even though it was the first time they had tried it that way it sounded fantastic and Mrs. Cambell was gleaming. For about an hour and a half they practiced all the new songs she gave them, and then quit for the evening.

"Now practice these over and over until we meet again Thursday evening." They all waved goodbye to each other and headed home. Kim said goodbye to Rachel and headed on home.

CHAPTER 9

When Kim made it home, she went straight to her room. As she walked toward her bed, she thought she heard sobbing. "Amber, are you ok?" She sat down on Amber's bed.

"I don't know," Amber said.

"I don't know," Amber said again, as she rolled over and wiped her eyes. "I just don't know what I'm going to do. I've got a boyfriend and he's in trouble."

"Yes, I know," Kim said. "I know that."

Amber looked surprised. "Everybody knows it, Amber. It's no secret," Kim replied. "What's his name?"

"Jake," Amber whispered, wanting to make sure Vickie didn't hear her.

"What kind of trouble is he in?" Kim moved over to her bed and started getting her pajamas on.

Amber didn't want to tell Kim that it had to do with drugs, so she lied and said, "He was accused of stealing something, but I know him, he wouldn't steal anything from anybody."

Kim knew Amber was lying, but she didn't want to confront her with it, because she already so upset and didn't need any more problems than she already had.

The next morning came quickly, and Kim was off to meet Rachel on the way to school. Amber started for school, but changed her mind and decided to ditch school. She wanted to see if she could find out what was going to happen to Jake. She headed for the police station where she saw him the last time. She walked into the station and up to the desk sergeant.

"Is Jake Moran here?" she asked. The officer looked at her. Then he smiled, remembering her from the last time she came. It isn't often a girl as attractive as Amber walked into a police station.

"Well, well," he said, "so you've come to see your scumbag friend Jake again, huh? Haven't you learned your lesson yet?"

"That's none of your business," Amber responded. "I just want to see him. Now can I or not?"

"Just wait here," he said. "I'll have to go check with the officer in charge of that particular case to see if it's ok." He got up, walked down the hall, and disappeared into a room. When he came out he had a piece of paper in his hand. "Here," he said, handing her the paper. "Walk down that hall," he pointed, "and turn left at the end. Walk till you see a guard at the cell and give it to him and he'll let you in. They'll only give you about fifteen minutes," he added.

Amber rushed down the hall, turned the corner, went up to the guard, and handed him the paper. The guard looked at her for a minute captivated by her beauty. He unlocked the main door, they went through, and he locked it behind them. Then they walked down a long hall. As they walked, the guard looked her over again, wondering how a girl so pretty could have anything to do with the likes of Jake Moran. Of course he had no way of knowing Amber was a drug addict. They finally reached Jake's cell and he opened it and let her in.

"You only have fifteen minutes," he told her, as he locked the door and then walked back down the hall. She jumped into Jake's arms kissing and hugging him with all her might. As she stood hugging and kissing him she all of a sudden realized something. No matter how bad Jake was, he was all she had in the world. Her mother and father were dead. She had a younger sister, but that wasn't the same. She loved Jake very much and she would do anything for him, no matter what it was.

"What are you doing here?" Jake asked. "How did you know, who told you?"

Amber put her finger over his lips to stop him from talking. Then she said, "I was hiding in the building when I heard some men come and arrest you. I stayed hidden until everybody was gone." The scared look came on her face. "What are they going to do to you, Jake? Are you going to be in here a long time?"

"I don't know," he said. "Right now I'm caught. They've set the bail so high, there's no way I can raise that amount of money. That was four thousand dollars worth of coke they took off me and it isn't paid for yet. In fact, that is my biggest problem: how I'm going to pay for it."

Amber could tell by the strain on his face he was really scared. She had never seen Jake scared before and it frightened her. "Is there anything I can do?" she asked.

"Not right now," he said, "but keep close contact in case I need you, ok?"

"I'll do anything you want me to, Jake, no matter what it is," she said. "You are all I have in the world and I love you very much." She then began crying and Jake took her in his arms and held her.

"Everything will be all right," he said. "Don't worry about me. I'll beat this somehow."

As they sat and comforted each other, the guard returned and said, "Your time is up."

Amber kissed Jake again, hugged him tight, said goodbye and walked out of his cell. The guard led her back out through the main door and locked it.

Amber left the police station and headed home, scared and worried. As Amber walked slowly down the street, she glanced across the way and saw Paul talking to two men. One man was black, very short and thin. The other was white, tall and very husky. They were so engrossed in what they were talking about that Paul didn't see Amber walking down the other side of the street. I wonder what he's up to, she thought. It can't be anything good. There's something evil about him, she thought, and it bothered her that he was hanging around the house more and more. It was too early in the day to go home yet. School wasn't out yet and she didn't want to be in the house with Vickie any more than she had to. She went down to the city park and walked around, then sat down, she was very anxious. An hour or so passed, and while she was sitting on a bench, she happened to look up and saw the same two men Paul was talking to downtown. It made her nervous for some reason so she decided to go home. As she walked by them they didn't look at her but it still made her feel very uncomfortable. She then hurried home very quickly.

Vickie was working on the books for her drug business when Amber walked in the door. She quickly closed them. As she got up to put them away, Vickie said, "Why are you home so early?" Amber completely ignored her as she went in her bedroom and slammed the door shut.

At that moment, Amber didn't really care what Vickie was doing. She went into her room, flung herself down on the bed, half sobbing, worrying about what was going to happen to Jake. She eventually fell asleep.

School was just letting out, and Kim and Rachel were walking down the sidewalk, when Jeff caught up with them.

"Are you going with me Friday?" he asked.

"You really want me to go, don't you?" Kim responded.

"Well, yes, or I wouldn't have asked you," he said.

"Ok," Kim said. "I'll go out with you, but don't come to my house. I'll meet you at the theater, Ok?"

"That's fine," he said. "How about seven o'clock?"

"That's good," Kim said as they crossed the street, leaving Jeff standing on the corner.

As they reached the other side of the street, Rachel laughed and said, "Wow, that's sure going to get everybody talking, especially Rosie. She thinks she's got him wrapped around her finger. Is she going to be shocked!" Kim just smiled as they walked on towards Rachel's house.

The next morning as Kim and Rachel were entering the school, a group of girls rushed to them and all tried to talk at once. One said, "We heard about your date with Jeff." Another said, "How did you do it?" Yet another said, "Since you're an underclassman, you know Juniors and Seniors don't go out with underclassmen."

"You are so lucky," another added. "I'd give my right arm for a date with him."

"You'd give more than that," another said and everyone started laughing.

Kim threw her hands up and said, "Wait a minute, how did you find out so fast?"

"Johnny told me," one girl answered.

"Bobby told me," another added.

"Danny told me," said another.

Well, Kim thought to herself, Jeff didn't waste any time telling everybody, did he?

When the crowd dispersed, Kim saw a girl across the way staring at them very hard. It was none other than Rosie. Rosie then walked over to them. "I want to talk to you," she said angrily. "Alone," she said, looking at Rachel.

"I'll see you later," Rachel said, taking the hint.

Rosie then focused her hard glare on Kim. "I heard you're stepping out with my boyfriend," she said as her anger was growing.

"I didn't know he was your boyfriend," Kim said as she turned her back on her to put something in her locker.

Rosie was a rather cute girl, but was not nearly as pretty as Kim. She grabbed Kim's shoulder and spun her around. "Don't you turn your back on me. I'm giving you fair warning, girl: you stay away from Jeff. You understand, sweetie?"

Kim weighed the situation carefully and said, "That's up to Jeff, not me. He asked me to go out and I'm going out with him!"

Rosie grabbed Kim by the front of her blouse and drew her hand back to hit her when someone grabbed her arm. She turned and saw Amber, holding her arm, glaring at her. Amber was about the same size as Rosie, but every girl in school knew Amber was no one to fool with when you got her upset.

Amber said, "Either you let her go or I'm going to beat you senseless."

Rosie slowly let Kim loose. Then Amber said, "If you ever lay another hand on my sister, I'll make sure you're so ugly, no guy will ever ask you out again." Rosie glared at Amber and then slowly started walking down the hallway looking back every now and then.

Amber then turned to Kim. "You really started some excitement around here. Is it true, you're going out with Jeff?"

"Yes," Kim said with a smile.

"You're awful young to be going out, you know. If dad were alive, I don't think he would allow it, especially since you're only a tenth grader."

"I'm going out with him," Kim said sternly.

"Ok, ok," Amber said, "I'm not going to try to talk you out of it. Amber then smiled and said, "I think every girl in school likes that guy. How did you hook him?"

"I don't know," Kim answered. "He kept asking me and I finally said yes."

"You mean you made him ask more than once?" Amber laughed.

"He was too cocky the first time he asked me. You said every girl in school likes him; how come you don't?" Kim asked.

"I've got a boyfriend," Amber answered. "He's much more mature than Jeff," she added. "Listen Kim, Jeff's got a smooth tongue. Don't let him talk you into doing anything you don't want to do. Do you understand what I'm talking about? I know his type pretty well."

"I won't," Kim answered.

"We better get moving," Amber said as she looked at the time, "or were going to be late for class. One more time for me and I'm in big trouble.

They both rushed off in different directions heading for their class. As Kim went and sat down next to Rachel, she said, "talk about making a big deal out of nothing; I can't believe the hype about a dumb date." Then the teacher started the class.

CHAPTER 10

School was over and Kim and Rachel were walking towards home. Rachel noticed that Kim had been quiet for a spell and she wondered what might be wrong. Finally Kim spoke up and said, "Rachel, who's God?"

The question caught Rachel by surprise. "Well," she said, "God is the creator of all things: the heavens, the earth, the solar system we live in, the galaxies and everything else that we don't even know about yet."

"How do you know that's all true?" Kim asked.

"By faith, I believe everything in the Bible is true."

"What's faith?" Kim asked.

"Well," Rachel said, "faith is believing God is real even though you can't see him. Faith strengthens our belief in the things we hope for, the things we trust will happen with God's help."

"Oh," Kim said. "Tell me, was Adam the first man on earth?"

"Well," Rachel began, "I don't know if Adam was the first man on earth, but I do know he was the first man created in God's image, which means he has a soul and a spirit which makes him superior over all things on earth. You see without a soul, which I believe is our rational mind, and a spirit to communicate with God, you would be like an animal. If there were men on the planet before Adam, that's probably what they were like. They probably lived in trees and caves or whatever, who can tell?"

Kim was quiet for a few minutes and then said, "Well, they're teaching us evolution in school that man came from an animal. You being a Christian can't believe both."

"Evolution is definitely not true as far as I'm concerned," Rachel answered.

"Why?" Kim asked.

"Because," Rachel began, "to make a long story short, they teach that through nature, man evolved from an animal over millions of years. Yet all the other animals stayed the same. That's ridiculous! If it was true, how man came into being, then all the cows, horses, elephants and whatever would now be evolved into something just as intelligent as we are. It basically teaches that we ate elephant brains millions of years ago and that's why we're so intelligent. Well, I've been to the zoo and to a circus and I've yet to see an elephant as smart as I am."

Kim laughed at that statement. Kim was quiet again for a moment, then said, "you sure dumped a load on me, ya know that?" She looked a little bewildered from it all.

"I'm sorry," Rachel said. "I didn't mean to; I get carried away sometimes when I get on the subject of evolution. It burns me up how people can believe that stuff."

"That's all right," Kim said. "I asked for it." They reached Rachel's house and went in. Kim said, "Oh, there's choir practice tonight. I better call Vickie and let her know where I'm at so there won't be any problems later."

Seven o'clock finally came and choir practice started. The first song they sang was *In the Garden* with Kim singing the lead and the choir backing her up. After it was over Kim headed home.

Friday morning finally rolled around. Kim got up and got ready for school. She went in the kitchen to get something to eat. As she sat there, she said to Vickie, "I have a date tonight with a boy from school. I thought I should tell you."

Before Vickie could answer, the phone rang and she answered it. It was Paul. As she talked to Paul, she looked and saw Kim still waiting for an answer. She said, "Yeah, yeah, just get out of here and leave me alone." Kim ran out of the house, tickled because she didn't have any trouble with Vickie. She met Rachel and they went on to school.

Jeff came up to her in his study hall and asked her if she was still going to go. Kim affirmed it and out of the corner of her eye, she could see Rosie glaring at her.

School was out and Kim went home with Rachel just for a while. Then she decided it was time to go home and get ready for her first date. She showered and put on one of the prettiest dresses she had. She was extra careful putting her make-up on for she wanted everything to be perfect.

Kim left the house and started walking toward the theater, when she saw Jeff, standing on the corner. "I thought we were supposed to meet at the theater," Kim said, a little angry.

"I know," said Jeff, "but I wanted to walk with you."

"Why?" Kim asked.

"Why?" he responded. "Just because I wanted to, that's why. How come you didn't want me to pick you up at your house? That way, I would have driven my car, and we wouldn't have to walk."

"I like to walk," said Kim. "Besides, I'm not ready to get in a car with you yet. I don't know you that well."

"Okay," he said as he shook his head in wonderment.

Kim did not want Jeff coming to the house because she didn't want him to meet Vickie. She was ashamed of her. All her drinking and the way she talked and especially how she treated her.

As they walked along, Jeff said, "I'm sorry about your father dying a while back. I heard he was a pretty good guy."

"Thank you," Kim returned with a slight quiver in her voice, for she hadn't thought about her father for quite a while. "My mother was wonderful, too, but she died a long time ago."

"Man, that really stinks. That's too bad. I heard your step-mother, Vickie—isn't that her name?—is kind of a bitch," he said. Kim was startled. She didn't know anyone knew that. The only thing she could figure is that Amber must have been talking about her at school.

"Where did you hear that?" she asked.

"Around school," he said.

"That's what I thought," Kim said. "Well, you're right, she's terrible to live with. It's pretty hard for me and Amber, but we'll live through it I guess."

They arrived at the theater and Jeff went and bought the tickets. They walked in, he bought a box of popcorn and two sodas to take with them, and then they went in and sat down way in the back of the theater. The movie started and they watched intently as they enjoyed their popcorn and sodas. When the movie was about half over, Jeff reached over and kissed her on the cheek. Then he put his arm around her and pulled her over to him. He turned her head and kissed her on the lips. It was the first time Kim had ever been kissed by a boy. Her father had kissed her before but it wasn't the same. He kissed her again on the lips and then on the neck. Kim was experiencing feelings she never felt before and she liked it. Then she put her arms around his neck and kissed him back. As they sat and made-out, Jeff said, "You know, I've had my eye on you ever since you were a freshman, but I knew I'd have to wait till you got a little older. I always dreamed about what it would be like to hold you and kiss you like this."

Kim didn't say anything and she was shocked that someone felt about her like that. That is, if he's not just feeding her a line.

"In fact," Jeff continued, "I remember the first time I ever saw you. You were in eighth grade and you came by the high school with your dad to pick up your sister. I thought you were the prettiest girl I'd ever seen."

Kim laughed, and he said, "No, I really mean it."

"I'll bet you do," Kim responded.

"So help me God," he said. "I know you've probably heard a lot of things around the school about me, but I feel different about you, honest! There have been lots of girls I've liked, but not like you."

Kim simply did not know what to say. She just looked at him and smiled. "I hope you believe me," he said, and kissed her on the tip of her nose. The movie finally ended, but they were so engrossed with each other they only saw about half of it.

They left the theater and started towards Kim's house. As they walked he held her hand. Then Kim spoke up. "You know, your friend Rosie gave me a rough time because you asked me out. She kind of scared me at first, but Amber came to my rescue."

Jeff turned red in the face. "That bitch! Just because I took her out once she tells everybody in school I'm her boyfriend. She acts like she owns me. I thought it was funny, but I see it's not funny anymore. I'll have a talk with her."

"No," Kim said, "it's over now. She won't bother me any more. She's afraid of Amber, so I don't think there will be any more problems."

As they got closer to Kim's house, Kim noticed Jeff was getting fidgety and sort of nervous. "Is anything wrong?" she asked.

"No," he said. When they reached the steps of her house, he kissed her and said, "Well, I gotta go. I'll give you a call tomorrow," and he rushed off.

Kim was puzzled; first he tells me how much he likes me and then he can't get away from me fast enough, she thought. She shrugged her shoulders and went on in the house. She walked into the kitchen and saw Vickie sitting at the table drinking and puffing on a cigarette.

"Well," Vickie said, "how was your date? Did he get in your pants?"

"No!" Kim answered angrily as her face turned red.

"No?" Vickie said with a grin. "Did he try?"

"No!" Kim said as she ran out of the kitchen and to her room.

Vickie laughed as she got up and staggered to the cupboard to get another drink, for she was very drunk. Amber was getting ready for bed as Kim came running into the bedroom. Kim said, "That bitch has a dirty mind. I hate her, I hate her." She flung herself on the bed.

Amber thought for a minute, then said, "I still don't think we've seen how wicked she can be."

Saturday morning came and Kim got up early. She wanted to get her work done and get out of the house as soon as she could. She just couldn't stand to be around Vickie and she knew it would probably be noon before she got up. She cleaned all the dishes, washed the top of the refrigerator, washed the table and then scrubbed the floor. Then she went in her room, made her bed, took a shower, got dressed and left the house.

As she was walking down the street towards Rachel's, Jeff pulled up in his car. "Where you going?" he asked. "It's almost noon; we could go down to Denny's and get something to eat."

"Ok," Kim said. "I am getting kind of hungry." Kim ran around the car, opened the door and got in.

At Denny's they found a booth they liked and sat down. The waitress came and they ordered. While they sat waiting for their food, Jeff asked, "What are you doing tonight?"

"I don't know," Kim answered.

"Want to go for a ride?" he asked.

"Where?" Kim said.

"Oh, I don't know, just riding. No special place. We'll just cruise around, just for something to do." Jeff responded.

"Maybe," Kim answered. "I'll call and let you know."

"How come you can't tell me now?" he asked.

"Because I haven't made up my mind yet," she said. "I have a commitment with Rachel to practice some songs we're going to be singing in the choir at church."

"You're kidding me," he said, astonished.

"No," Kim answered. "What's wrong with that? I like to sing. Besides Rachel is my best friend and I can't desert her."

"Ok, ok," he said, and then Jeff got fidgety like he did last night and said, "I'll be right back," and he went in the men's room. Their food came and he wasn't back yet. Kim didn't like to eat cold food, so she started eating. Jeff finally came back, didn't say anything, just sat down and started eating. He seemed much calmer now, Kim thought. They finished and left.

Jeff drove her to Rachel's house and kissed her on the cheek and said, "Call me if you can go, ok?"

"Ok," Kim answered. Jeff drove off, waving back at her as he left.

Kim went up and knocked on the door. Rachel's mother answered it. She was happy to see Kim; the more Kim was around, the more she liked her. "Rachel's in the back yard, pulling weeds out of the flower garden," she said.

Kim walked through the house and out the back door to where Rachel was. "Need some help?" Kim asked.

"Yeah," Rachel answered, a little out of breath and wiping her forehead. As Kim helped her pull weeds, she said, "Jeff asked me to go riding with him tonight, but I told him we had to practice our songs for choir."

"Do you want to go with him?" Rachel asked.

"Yeah," Kim said, "but that's ok, we need to practice."

"I'm just about done," Rachel said. "We could practice early and then you could go. Tell me what happened last night? Did he kiss you?"

"Yes," Kim answered.

"Did he put his arms around you?" Rachel asked.

"Yes," Kim answered.

Then Rachel got a serious look on her face and said, "Did he try to fool around?"

"No," Kim responded.

"No?" Rachel said in surprise. "That's not what I've heard about him."

"He didn't even try," Kim repeated.

"Would you if he did?"

"I don't know," Kim answered.

"Kim, am I your best friend?" Rachel asked.

"Yes," Kim said.

"Then as your friend I'll be straight with you: don't do it no matter how you feel. You'll be very sorry later."

"Why?" Kim asked. "Everyone does it," she added.

"Well, I don't," Rachel responded, "and I won't till I meet the right man when I get older and get married."

Then Rachel thought a minute and said, "Just because everybody does it, doesn't make it right!"

Kim didn't answer as she pondered everything Rachel said.

CHAPTER 11

When they finished with the weeds, they went in and washed their hands, went to the piano and started practicing. It was early evening when they finished. Rachel's mother again invited Kim to stay and have supper with them. Kim said, "Well, I have to make a phone call first."

Mrs. Harding said, "Ok, use the phone on Jim's desk."

Kim picked up the phone and dialed Jeff's number. "Hello," someone answered at the other end. It was a woman's voice, so Kim assumed it was his mother.

"Can I speak to Jeff, please?" she asked.

"Who is calling?" the woman asked.

"Oh, my name is Kim. Remember. I called yesterday."

"Oh yes," she responded. "Well, Jeff's not here, he left about fifteen minutes ago and I don't know when he will be back."

"Oh," Kim said dejectedly. "Just tell him I called."

"All right," his mother said, "I'll tell him. Goodbye," and she hung up the phone. Kim did the same, very disappointed.

"I'll stay for supper," Kim said as she sat down. As they ate Kim wondered why he didn't wait for her to call. After all, she told him she would. She then was angry with him. Then she thought, maybe he had a good reason. I'll wait and see what he says tomorrow as she put it out of her mind for now.

Meanwhile it was slowly getting dark. Amber sat on the steps of the front porch, staring down at the ground, when she noticed two legs in front of her. She looked up and saw Jimbo looking down at her. "Hi," he said in a sad sort of way.

"What are you doing here?" Amber asked.

"Oh, with Jake gone, I...I just...well, just don't know what to do. I mean, I feel lost I guess. Jake's the only friend I got. I'm worried about what's going to happen to him. I don't have anyone to hang out with, so I, well, I thought I'd come and see you. It's all right, isn't it?" he asked as he looked at her searchingly.

Amber saw the loneliness in his face and she thought she was just as lonely, without Jake. "Sure," she said. "It's all right."

A big smile spread across Jimbo's face as she said that. "Oh, thanks," he replied. "I promise I won't be annoying. I just need someone to talk to. I'll keep you informed about what's happening to Jake. I go down there and check most everyday to see what's going on. If you ever need to go anywhere, just call me. My car ain't new, but it runs good."

"Thanks," Amber said with a slight smile, standing and touching his hand as a gesture of friendship. She looked at Jimbo's car and then said, "You want to take a ride, maybe down to the drive-in and get a soda or something?"

"Sure," Jimbo said excitedly. "Sure, sure." He hurried to his car and opened the door for her.

They drove into the drive-in and parked. The carhop came and they both ordered a soda. While they were waiting, another car pulled in along side of them. There were four young men in it, and they apparently knew Jimbo. The one nearest rolled his window down and hollered, "Hey Jimbo, you taking Jake's place with his girl? Ha, ha. Have you taken her to bed yet?" He laughed again.

Jimbo got out of the car, quickly opened the door on the other car and with one hand, pulled the young man out. Then still holding him with one hand, he punched him hard in the stomach again and again. Then he lifted him high in the air, still with one hand and started to hit him again, when Amber screamed, "Don't, Jimbo, you're going to kill him. Let him go. It's all right, it's all right."

Jimbo let him drop to the ground. Then he bent down and said, "You don't talk bad about my friends, do you hear me? You don't talk bad or I'll kill you, do you hear me?"

The man just shook his head yes, for he couldn't talk because of the pain and couldn't catch his breath. The other three men just froze in their seats. They never knew Jimbo was that strong and they never saw him ever get mad like that. They had always seen him as a big dumb, happy-go-lucky type of guy. They all thought, without speaking, that even if they got out and jumped him, he would probably pound all their heads in. They weren't going to find out. Finally, the man on the ground managed to get up. He staggered to the door of the car and got in. The driver burned rubber backing up and burned rubber again as he took off down the street.

Jimbo slowly got back in his car, frowning as he looked at Amber. Amber said with a smile, "It's all right, you couldn't help it. One thing for sure: they'll never bother you again."

After they finished their drinks, Jimbo drove her back to her house. Amber got out, said goodbye as he drove off. Walking towards the house she saw Kim coming up the sidewalk so she sat down on the steps and waited for her. Kim finally arrived but didn't say anything as she sat down on the steps also.

"What's the matter?" Amber asked. "You look down."

"Nothing," Kim answered. "I just need something to do I guess. Is Vickie in there?"

"I don't know and I don't really care," Amber answered. They sat for a while saying nothing, then got up and went in the house to their room, turned on the TV and just laid back. An hour passed and it was pretty dark out when they heard a car pull up out front. Kim thought it might be Jeff so she looked out the window with Amber looking over her shoulder. It wasn't, but they recognized the car. It was Paul; even in the dark they could tell. But no one got out so they went back to watching TV.

Paul and Vickie were in the car, arguing heatedly. "I'm telling you again," Vickie said, "I don't want you involving Amber. She lives in my house and it's clean as far as the police are concerned.

My husband was a well known man with integrity. Everybody liked him, and nobody suspects anything. You've been hauled in too many times. Even if they've never pinned anything on you, you're watched by the cops. You can find enough little whores without her. I don't give a damn about her, but if the cops ever tied her with you, then they would start watching my house. Right now I have a perfect set up for moving drugs with no suspicion and I'm not going to let you ruin it, so hands off her, do you understand?" she said, fuming.

Paul wasn't giving up easy, for he had personal interest in Amber, besides making a street prostitute out of her. But Vickie was too strong in her convictions right now, so he thought he would let it lay for a while. "Ok, ok," he said loudly, "but I'm telling you she'd make a good one. I'm not going to find many girls that are as attractive as her, do you understand that? They have to be alluring enough to draw the men."

"I said no," Vickie said again loudly. "No, no, no! You better get out of here; you've been around too long already."

"Why? It's dark," Paul responded.

"I don't care," Vickie said. "I don't want some cop driving by and seeing your car. Next time drive in the alley. Don't ever come during the day. It's too dangerous, you might be spotted."

"Right," he said. He reached over and kissed her on the cheek as if he really didn't want to and Vickie sensed it.

She said as she got out of the car, "You've got your mind on that kid in there, huh?"

"No," Paul said, acting puzzled.

Vickie just glared at him and then went in the house as he drove off. She heard the TV going in the girls' room as she walked through the house. She went in the kitchen, sniffed some coke, and then got out a bottle of bourbon and poured herself a large glass full, sat down at the table and lit a cigarette.

Sunday morning came and Kim was up at the crack of dawn, got in the shower, dressed and was on her way to Rachel's house. When she got there, Rachel wasn't even ready yet. "Wow! You're early," Rachel said as she opened the door, yawning.

"Sorry," Kim said. "I wanted to get away from the house before Vickie woke up."

"Good," Rachel said, "you can have break-fast with me. I'm the only one around who eats breakfast on Sunday morning, and almost any morning."

That really sounded good to Kim, she was starving. They headed for the kitchen, Rachel stopped at the refrigerator, opened the door and got out a package of bacon. She picked up a knife and cut the package open. As she put several slices of bacon in the skillet, she said, "How do you like your eggs, huh?"

"Scrambled, I guess," Kim answered.

"Grab about six out of the fridge," Rachel replied. Rachel then broke them in a bowl and beat them with a whisk. Then she turned to Kim and said, "What would you like to drink?"

Kim thought for a minute then said, "I guess milk will be ok."

"I'm having coffee," Rachel replied. "Don't say anything about it around the church," she said dryly. "Some people think it's a sin," and then she giggled.

Kim sat down and watched Rachel at the stove, busy turning the bacon and stirring the eggs. She put coffee grounds and water in the pot and plugged it in. Kim was amazed at how well Rachel had everything under control, and the food smelled so good, she couldn't remember the last time she enjoyed the smell of breakfast. Finally she said, "Hurry up, Rachel, the smell of that stuff is driving me out of my mind. I'm starved."

Rachel looked at her, grinning, and said, "I'm hurrying, I'm hurrying. Set the table, would you? You know where everything is."

Kim got up immediately and began setting the table. By the time Kim was finished, the food was done. Kim poured the coffee and milk, while Rachel served the food. "What's in store for this morning," Kim asked when Rachel finished praying over the food.

"Well, first we'll practice for about an hour with the choir and then go to Sunday school, and then to church." They finished eating; Rachel got dressed and was then ready to go. While Kim waited, she stared out the window, wondering where her life was going. Then Rachel heard her speak out. "Who am I? Where am I going? Why was I born? Why did my dad have to die and why is life so hard and full of pain?" she said slowly. Rachel put her hand gently on her shoulder and said, "Come on, let's go," and out the door they went.

It was unusually warm for that early in the morning, so they didn't wear any coats or sweaters. They arrived at the church and went around to the side building where the choir room was to practice. As they walked in, Mrs. Cambell greeted them with a big smile and said, "Good morning!" as they sat down. Kim wondered as she sat, why can't the teachers at school be as nice as Mrs. Cambell, instead of like a bunch of jerks, always growling. They don't even smile and when they do, it's so phony. Then Mrs. Cambell called out to the choir to pay attention and they began practicing.

It was 12:30 when church was over and Kim walked Rachel home. Then she headed home herself.

CHAPTER 12

Meanwhile back at the house, Amber was just starting to wake up. She was twisting and rolling as Molly was on the bed, sticking her nose down under the pillow trying to get to Amber's face to lick it. She was whining and jumping around on Amber and all over the bed. She let out a bark and Amber woke up quickly, grabbed Molly and put her hand over her mouth and whispered, "Shhhh, be quiet, Vickie will hear you."

But it was too late. Vickie had heard Molly and came storming into Amber's bedroom, yelling. "You got that damn dog in the house again. I warned you, didn't I?" as she grabbed one of

Amber's shoes and threw it at Molly, chasing her out of the house.

"You better not hurt her!" Amber yelled, hurrying to put her robe on and chasing after them. "She hasn't done anything to you. Leave her alone!"

Vickie then turned her rage from the dog and attacked Amber. She came rushing back in the house, and shoved Amber backwards saying, "I'll do what I want to that damn dog, do your hear me? I'll kill it if I want to, do you hear me?" she yelled.

Then Amber lost her senses as her anger rose. She looked Vickie straight in the eyes and said, "You hurt that dog and you'll be sorry."

That sent Vickie into a rage. She charged Amber, hit her, and knocked her to the floor, screaming, "Don't you ever talk to me like that again, you hear me? I said, do you hear me?" she screamed again.

Amber got up and said, "Yes, I hear you, but you better not hurt our dog or so help me, Kim and I will get even no matter what you do." Then she turned and went into her room.

Vickie stood and watched her go, wondering if she should call her bluff or just drop it for now, when Kim came in the front door. Kim could tell by the look on Vickie's face that something had happened but she didn't say a word as she headed into the bedroom. Vickie stared after her. Kim closed the door behind her, walked up to Amber, and noticed she was wiping blood from her mouth where Vickie had hit her.

"What happened?" Kim asked.

"Molly barked and Vickie caught her in bed with me," Amber answered. Amber was quiet for a minute and then said, "If she hurts our dog, so help me, I'll kill her. I'll kill her, so help me."

Kim saw a look in Amber's eyes she had never seen before and she realized that Amber probably hated Vickie more than she herself did, if that was possible. Kim decided to help Amber. She slowly opened the door and went into the kitchen. Vickie had gone to her bedroom. Kim quietly went out the back door looking for Molly. She found her hiding by the steps. Kim picked her up and took her over to her little dog house which her father had built for Molly two years before. She tied her up with the rope that was attached to it then she scampered back into the house to her bedroom.

Amber was staring off into space as if she didn't know anyone was near. Kim just stood and looked at her for a couple of minutes, thinking of something she could say. Finally she said, "Amber, what are we going to do?"

Amber turned slowly and looked at her with a tear in her eye. "I don't know. I guess we'll have to wait till Mr. Jenkins calls and tells us what to do." She was silent for a moment and then continued, "That's all I know to do. I hope it's soon, because I don't know how much more I can take of her. Everything bad is happening to me." She started crying. "What else can go wrong?" she sobbed, becoming hysterical and out of control. Kim sat down beside her again and put her arm around her, feeling about as helpless as she's ever felt about anything. If only she could help her sister. She knew her problems went beyond Vickie. She knew Amber was doing drugs now and she knew that her boyfriend Jake was in real trouble. She hoped Amber was strong enough to handle all the problems they were facing.

It was Thursday and time for two days of finals, with one week of school left. Kim did very well on her tests but Amber struggled. She messed around most of the year and never put in much effort, especially since she had been on drugs. Finally the week past and it was Friday, Graduation Day. Amber was in her bedroom putting on her cap and gown when Vickie opened the door and walked in. She didn't say anything at first, she just walked around while Amber watched her.

Then she said, "So, you're finally getting out of school, eh? My, my, ain't we somebody. Well understand one thing," she continued, "just because you're no longer in school doesn't mean you can come and go as you please. You will still answer to me, understand? I'm still in control."

Amber didn't say anything. Then Vickie said in a loud voice, "Did you hear me?"

"I heard you," Amber answered.

Vickie left the room and Amber continued fussing with her gown so it would look right. Kim had just returned home and as she walked into the bedroom she yelled softly, "Wow, do you look great! Very pretty."

Amber smiled and said, "You're just jealous because you're not graduating."

"You're absolutely right. I really wish I was, too, so I could get out of this place." Then Kim said in a half whisper, so Vickie wouldn't hear her, "What are going to do after graduation? Are you going to move out or what?"

"Not on your life," Amber responded. "Not till we find out from Mr. Jenkins what is going to happen to our home and money. I wish it didn't take so long for all the details to work out. Who knows, maybe the court will throw her out. Boy, wouldn't that be a laugh!" and they both started laughing out loud. Vickie could hear them and wondered what was so funny.

Kim got dressed and put on her make-up. Then she and Amber headed to school, for the ceremonies, even though it was still a little early. They wanted to get out of the house as quick as possible. Vickie had no plans of attending the graduation and she would be out of their sight for at least another day.

As they reached the bleachers at the football field they were surprised to see most of the graduating class was also early. The students were mingling among everybody. Marsha ran up to Amber and stopped her as Kim continued to walk on. "Isn't this exciting," she said. "I can't wait to get out of here, can you?"

"No," Amber said kind of half smiling.

Marsha was a tall girl, a little on the heavy side and plain looking, with brown hair and blue eyes. Amber and Marsha had known each other since they were very small. She was the only other girl in school that Amber seemed to get along with, although they were as different as night and day. Amber was not dumb, but because of her drug addiction, she did not achieve; Marsha, on the other hand, was a straight A student and class president. Her parents pushed her very hard and expected her to be perfect. She resented it, but there was nothing she could do about it. Over the years, she developed a false personality, always being nice and always saying the right things to please her parents and the teachers. But when she was around Amber, she could let her hair down and be herself since she trusted Amber and felt comfortable around her.

"I had my speech all written and when my father read it, he practically re-wrote it. It's nothing like I really wanted to say. Fact is, the one I wrote wasn't really what I wanted to say either. But I have to please mommy and daddy or it's impossible to live with them, you know?" she said in a sarcastic way.

Amber looked Marsha straight in the eyes and said, "Why don't you say what you want to say. You're a big girl now. When are you going to stand up for yourself? Are you always going to buckle under to everybody all the time? Be yourself, Marsha, be yourself," she repeated. "I've known you almost all my life; you're always trying to please everybody. The hell with everybody! Just be who you want to be."

Marsha just stared at Amber for a minute and then shaking nervously said, "I don't know if I can do that. Oh, I just don't know if I have the courage to say what I really think. I'm afraid they would run me off the platform if I did."

"So what!" said Amber. "They can't lock you up for saying what you think, can they? So your parents would get angry, who cares? It's your life and no one can live it for you."

Marsha, still very nervous over what Amber said, repeated, "Oh I just don't think I can do that Amber. I just can't," she repeated.

"Well just go up there and be phony," Amber said a little angry. Then Marsha sadly looked down at the ground.

Amber put her hand on Marsha's hands clasped in front of her and said, "I'm sorry, Marsha. You do what you think is best. Don't pay any attention to what I said. I haven't been myself lately. You just go up and do what you think you should do, ok?"

Marsha looked up and with a little smile and tears, walked away. Amber felt very bad about her words to Marsha and wished she hadn't opened her mouth.

As time passed, seeming like an eternity to the students, the principal, Mr. Frazer, and all the teachers involved in the graduation ceremonies, arrived and went up on the platform. People started getting everything ready such as checking out the microphones, making sure the diplomas were in the right order, and so on. The parents, relatives, friends, and etc. started filling the bleachers. Mr. Frazer walked to the microphone and said, "Will all the graduating students please take their places in line; we're ready to begin."

When they were ready the students walked up the steps in proper order to their seats. "Shhhh," one of the teachers whispered as they were sitting down. It seemed like time was standing still, waiting for the next phase of the program. They were fidgety and had the jitters as they sat and waited. All of a sudden Marsha jumped up, ran up to Mr. Frazer, and whispered something in his ear.

"What?" he said in a startled voice.

"Please," she said, "this is what I want to do. Please, please," she repeated over and over.

"Well," he said slowly, "I guess it would be all right."

Marsha took her seat, gripping her speech very nervously. Amber was watching her wondering what she was up to, but she sat too far away to ask her. The students were fidgety and bored as they sat waiting for things to begin. They were whispering and giggling and goofing off.

Finally it was time, and Mr. Frazer went to the microphone and said, "Good afternoon, ladies and gentlemen. I want to welcome you to graduation ceremonies. I'm especially proud of the class this year. This is the first time in the history of the school we've had three valedictorians in one graduating class." The crowd cheered and then was quiet again. Then Mr. Frazer continued. "I'll now introduce them to you." He turned, looked back at the students and said, "Our first valedictorian is Marsha Scott." Marsha stood up and the crowd cheered. Then he said, "George Polk." George stood up and the crowd cheered again. Then he said, "Delores Wimple." Delores stood and the crowd cheered again.

Then Mr. Frazer said, "At this point I would like to announce a slight change in our program." He smiled and continued, "Our class President normally would speak at this time but has requested to wait until after the diplomas are handed out. So let's begin."

Two of the teachers carried a small table with all the diplomas on it up to the microphone where Mr. Frazer was standing. As Mr. Frazer called the names, the teachers picked up a diploma and handed it to Mr. Frazer. Then as the students passed by, he handed them the diploma and shook their hand. It was a long grind and all two hundred and one students passed by, one at a time to get their diploma. The crowd would cheer after each name was called and Mr. Frazer handed them their priceless piece of paper. Finally the last diploma was handed out and all the students sat down and the crowd cheered again.

CHAPTER 13

Then it was time for Marsha to speak. Mr. Frazer went to the microphone again and said, "And now, finally, our class President, Marsha Scott, will make her presentation."

Marsha got up and walked to the microphone. She stood and waited till the crowd quit cheering. "Thank you, thank you," she said. She was quiet for a few seconds as she looked over the crowd from one end of the bleachers to the other. "I've always wondered what this moment would be like and now I know. I'm nervous," she said laughing, and the crowd laughed with her. "Today is the beginning of a new world for us. We go from here to make our way in life. Some of us will go on to college, some will become tradesmen, some nurses, some doctors, some attorneys, some dentists, and even some teachers," she said with a giggle. "One of my subjects in school this year was current events and politics, so at home I watched the news with my father." As she said this, her father puffed his chest out proudly. She continued, "Our nation has many problems today, problems they say we will inherit. Problems we will have to solve."

As she said these things, she could hear the whispers and groans from the students behind her saying "Oh no, here she goes again, up on her soap box preaching politics." She didn't like it. She was almost ready to cry when all of a sudden she wadded up her speech and threw it to the ground in front of the platform. Mr. Frazer was stunned as he stood way off at the end of the platform near the steps. He didn't know what to do. He started toward the microphone.

Marsha spoke up as she saw him coming. "No, I'm not finished," she said as she wiped a tear away. "You know, all my classmates and friends are around seventeen or eighteen years old. Most of our parents think because we're young that we don't know what's going on around us. It seems you think you are the only ones who know what's going on. You think all we really know is how to get up in the morning, go to school, come home, do our home work, eat, watch television and go to bed. On the weekends, go out on dates or whatever other interests we might have, right?" She said with a question. "Wrong," she said loudly. "I've got news for you. We're not stupid. We watch TV just like you do, and believe it or not, some of us read the newspaper. Since we were little kids, when the news comes on the tube, Dad, mom and I watch it too or leave the room until it's over so we can watch something else. But most of the time we'll just sit waiting impatiently until it's over. You know, I was just thinking, from the time we're about nine years old until you're my age, you've seen a lot of damn news. Now I'm not going to talk politics," she said as she turned and looked back at her classmates, "but I'm going to talk about politics, and you haven't heard anything yet." She then turned back and looked over the crowd. "We're all born with different gifts. Some of us are good mathematicians and could become a scientist or whatever, some of us have excellent mechanical skills and could become engineers in different fields. Others may have gifts to become doctors or lawyers. Ahhh, lawyers," she said with a drawl. "Did you know about 90% of our politicians are lawyers? But you see it takes more than just being a lawyer to make it in politics. You've got to have other gifts, too. Now if you've got a great line of bull you could run for Mayor or maybe Chief of Police. Now if you got a great line of bull and a damn good liar, you could probably run for the Senate or House of Representatives or even Governor. But ohhhh, if you're a good con artist, have a great line of bull, are a good liar with a teethy grin, and can talk intelligently in circles for hours without ever saying anything, you could run for President."

At that moment, the whole class stood up and cheered, waving their hats in the air as the principal was waving his arm for them to sit back down. Marsha then glanced at the principal thinking he was about to come over and stop her. But he didn't move, he realized this was a new breed of youth that was not going to be intimidated. He just nodded his head slightly for approval. Marsha smiled and turned back to the mic.

"We hear about all the gang problems, all the drug problems, how bad the national debt is with no way of curing it other then giving it lip service, because no one has any answers. If the politicians would keep their hands out of the cookie jar, it probably wouldn't be half the mess it is. Our nation is one of a few where a poor man or woman gets elected to a political office, and after a couple of terms, leaves or retires filthy rich beyond your or my wildest dreams. That's how the old game of payola is mastered. They tell us that when we graduate we will inherit the land and it will become our responsibility to take care of it and run it. I say, we don't want it. They made the mess so let them clean it up. If they can't do it then give it back to the Indians; they probably don't want it either."

She paused for a second and then said, "Hey, they might keep us confused some of the time, but not all the time." We hear about all the corruption in big business, banks, unions or whatever. I heard my mother say something to my father a while back that really stuck in my head. She said, we live in a time when greed is rampant. Everybody wants more! More money, more cars, more toys, and we keep getting greedier. It doesn't matter if you're rich or poor, this insatiable lust for more just keeps growing. Then she screamed in the microphone, "*WE ARE NOT STUPID!* That's all I have to say, Thank you." She quickly turned and went to her seat and sat down and started crying.

About that time, the whole class stood up and cheered, and threw their hats in the air. Then some of them went over to Marsha and hugged her, some kissed her on the cheek, and shook her hand. Tears came to her eyes as she finally felt accepted for the first time by her classmates.

Mr. Frazer put his hand on her shoulder and smiled as he looked at her face. "Marsha, I'm proud of you. I only hope you're strong enough to handle the repercussions."

Marsha smiled and said, "I'll be all right. I'm real now; I don't have to pretend or walk in confusion anymore." He smiled and walked away.

Amber went up to Marsha when she was able. She kissed her on the cheek, hugged her, smiled, and said, "You did real good Marsha, real good. You'll be all right now." Amber then walked down off the podium and just walked around aimlessly wishing Jake were there.

Kim searched through the crowd for Amber and finally found her. "Boy, that was some kind of speech," she said, looking bewildered.

Amber kind of smiled and said, "Yea, I'd hate to be in her shoes when she gets home. Boy, her dad is going to skin her alive, poor kid."

"Well," Kim said, "I'm going over to Rachel's house to practice our songs for Sunday."

"You sure are getting chummy with that church bunch, ain't you," Amber remarked. "Are you gonna be one of those Jesus freaks?" she said with a grim.

Kim looked puzzled. "What is a Jesus freak?" she asked.

"People that all they do is go around and talk about Jesus. Jesus this, and Jesus that," Amber answered.

That angered Kim and without thinking she responded, "That's better than being a druggy." And she ran off quickly when she realized what she said.

Amber was fuming over Kim's remark as she looked around to see if anyone had heard her. Amber walked across the street and as she reached the other side, a car pulled up. She turned and looked. It was Paul, Vickie's boyfriend.

"Hello," he said with a big smile. "Would you like a ride home?" he asked, trying very hard to be nice.

"No," said Amber and started walking down the street.

Paul drove very slowly along side of her and continued to try to talk her into getting in the car. "Look, all I want to do is give you a ride home, now what's wrong with that? You can trust me. After all, I know your mother."

"She's not my mother," Amber said angrily.

"Come on, get in the car," he said with a stern voice, "and I'll take you home. Now get in, I said."

"No," Amber answered, and she looked back. She could see Jimbo coming down the street in his car. She ran back past Paul's car and waved at Jimbo. He pulled over to the curb as soon as he saw her.

"Hi," he said, "what's cookin'?"

"I need a ride," Amber said, jumping in his car. "Let's get out of here." As they drove by Paul's car, Amber could see how angry he was.

"Who was that guy?" Jimbo asked.

"Just a snake," Amber answered.

"Jake's in real big trouble," Jimbo said as he glanced at Amber. "He needs an attorney and he ain't got enough money to hire one. I ain't got no money, what are we going to do?"

"I don't know," Amber answered. "I don't know." They finally reached Amber's house. As she got out, she turned and looked at Jimbo and said, "I'll think of something."

She went in the house as Jimbo drove off. Vickie was sitting at the table, smoking, with a drink in front of her "Well, you're out of school, heh? You better start looking for a job, kid. You're not going to stay around here and do nothing."

"What about the money Kim and I will be getting from the insurance company?" Amber asked.

"Don't you worry about that damn money," Vickie snorted. "You just get a job."

"By the way," Amber said as she started walking towards her room, "your boyfriend tried to pick me up on the street when I was coming home. He wouldn't leave me alone. I don't know what I would have done if Jimbo hadn't come along." She went into her room and closed the door.

Vickie was fuming as she drank and finally went into a rage. She stood up and slapped her glass off the table. It hit the floor and shattered. She kicked the chair over. "That son of a bitch," she screamed. She didn't care about Amber. She was just extremely jealous of Paul looking at any woman. "I could kill him," she screamed as she banged her fist on the table. She was so drunk she finally went into her bedroom and threw herself on the bed and went to sleep

Amber sat on the edge of her bed, wondering what she could do to help Jake. Her mind raced as she tried to come up with an answer. Then a light went off in her head. It was almost four o'clock. Maybe Mr. Jenkins was still in his office. She searched through her purse looking for his phone number, but she couldn't find it. She looked in her drawers in her dresser, but it wasn't there either. She was getting desperate. She went to her closet and started going through all the pockets of her clothes. She finally found it. She quietly opened her door and walked into the living room. Vickie was sleeping. She went to her bedroom door and listened. She could hear her snoring. She went back in her room. Vickie hadn't taken the phone out of their room yet. Amber dialed Mr. Jenkins' number. The phone rang and rang, but no answer.

She let it continue to ring and then finally someone said, "Mr. Jenkins' office. This is Mr. Jenkins."

"Mr. Jenkins, this is Amber Colden. I really need some help — that is my boyfriend needs help really bad. He's in jail and he needs an attorney, but he doesn't have any money. Is there anything you can do?" Before he could answer she went on. "You could take your fee out of the money you'll be sending to me and Kim until it's paid." Amber said that because she knew she and Kim would never see any money when Vickie got her hands on it anyway.

"Well, what kind of trouble is he in?" Mr. Jenkins asked.

"The police are trying to say that he was selling drugs to some boys, but I know he would never do anything like that," she lied. "He's innocent. Will you please help?" she pleaded.

"What's his name?" Mr. Jenkins asked.

"Jake Moran," Amber answered, "and they are holding him at the downtown precinct."

Mr. Jenkins paused for a minute then said, "All right, I'll try to get down there tomorrow and talk to him and see what I can do."

"Oh thank you," Amber said. "Thank you very much." She said goodbye to Mr. Jenkins and hung up her phone. She was excited, because she just knew Mr. Jenkins could save Jake. After all he was one of Daddy's best friends.

Meanwhile, Kim reached Rachel's house and knocked on the door. Rachel opened the door. "Oh, you're early. Come on in for a minute while I get ready."

Kim walked in and saw Pastor Harding sitting in the living room reading the paper. Mrs. Harding was in the kitchen bagging up some cookies for the girls to take with them. Kim followed Rachel into her room.

"Have you seen Jeff today?" Rachel asked.

"No," Kim said dejectedly.

"Well, I saw him," Rachel replied. "I'll tell you one thing: I don't care for the company he keeps. I saw him pick up a couple of guys in his car who got kicked out of school because they were involved in drugs. I hope he knows what he's doing."

"I don't think he would do drugs, do you?" Kim asked.

Rachel was silent for a second and then said, "No, I don't think so. I sure hope not. It would sure be a shame; he's so hot." Then she laughed. "Ok, I'm ready — let's go."

As they came out of Rachel's room her mother hollered from the kitchen. "I've got a bag of cookies you girls can take with you for all the kids, Ok?"

"Ok," Rachel answered back.

The boys and girls arrived for practice. Mrs. Cambell watched as Kim and Rachel walked in and sat down. She finally made up her mind that is the answer to her dilemma. She was going to build the choir around Kim. After all, she had the best voice and the ability to be very good, and she didn't have anyone else anyway.

The next morning Mr. Jenkins was driving to his office, deep in thought over Amber's phone call the day before, pleading for him to help Jake, her boyfriend. As he drove along he changed his mind and headed for the precinct to see Jake, and see if there was any way he could help, even though it was against his better judgment. His motive really was to help Amber.

He parked his car, got out and looked at the precinct and said, well here goes! He went in and walked up to the desk sergeant and asked, "Can I please see Jake Moran?"

The sergeant looked up at him and said, "Who are you?"

"My name is Jenkins and I have been retained as his attorney."

The sergeant just smiled and said, "Good Luck." He then called another policeman and told him to take Mr. Jenkins back to the holding area to see Jake. The holding area was a very small room with just one small table and chairs. It was very dismal. The officer brought Jake to the room where Jenkins was waiting. As Jake walked slowly into the room and over to the chair at the table he glared at Mr. Jenkins, wondering who he was and why he was there.

Jake sat down and said, "Who are you? What do you want with me?" He looked around the room not making any eye contact with Jenkins.

"I'm Dave Jenkins, Amber and Kim Colden's attorney. Amber wants me to try to help you with the situation you're in."

Before he could say another word, Jake butted in and said, "I don't need anybody's help; I can take care of myself."

"Do you have any family?" Jenkins asked.

"No," Jake said. "I can take care of myself, I don't need you."

Then Jenkins got angry. "Listen you punk — Amber's Father was one of my closest friends and I'm going to look after his two daughters the best I can. Now she asked me – no, she begged me — to see what I could do to help you. You can sit and make an ass of yourself and rot for all I care. Or you can talk to me and see what can be done. If you don't let someone help you with the mess you're in, you're going to end up behind bars for a long time."

That shook Jake up and a little fear showed on his face. Jake sat down and was quiet for a couple of seconds and then asked, "What can you do?"

"First," Jenkins said, "you have to tell me everything before I can do anything. I can't do anything without knowing what the score is. I know nothing about you. You have to talk, do you hear me? I need to know everything."

Jake was hesitant for a moment and then said, "Will this stay between you and me? I don't want Amber to know how much trouble I'm in."

"Amber knows more than you think," Jenkins said, "but if that's the way you want it then fine."

Jake got up and walked around a little and then sat down. He stuttered a bit as he started talking.

"A few years ago my dad ran off and left me and my mom. It was probably for the best. He used to come home drunk and beat the hell out of us. Anyway, I think he hated us. Mom worked two jobs to take care of me, but it was tough. I think she died of a broken heart. She was a sweet person; I loved her," he said, as a tear trickled down his cheek. "She did the best she could."

After that he was silent for a moment, and then spoke. "As I got older and seen how hard it was for her, I wanted to help. When I was in High School there were these guys who sold drugs to the kids and I seen the money they were making, so I got to know them and told them I wanted in. It took a long time because they had to make sure they could trust me. Once I was in, they gave me some contacts and I was in business. Within six months I was making good money and was able to help mom. I told her I had a cleaning job after school and she believed me. She never knew what I was really doing. Then she died when her heart just gave out. I got into it big time, I finally made contacts with some really big guys so I could bypass the smaller suppliers and make more money. Then I met Amber, and she was the best thing that happened to me. She didn't know then what I was doing. We love each other very much. I don't want her to get hurt, do you understand?"

Mr. Jenkins nodded yes, and then he got up and walked back and forth for a minute. Finally he said, "I think you should plead guilty and throw yourself on the mercy of the court. When the judge pronounces sentence, I will try to get you out on parole. It's a big gamble, but right now, it's all we got."

Jake stared at him for a moment and then said, "Is that the best we can do? What about my money; they took four thousand dollars off me."

Mr. Jenkins said, "If they believe it's drug money, which they will when you plead guilty, you'll never see that money again."

Jake looked scared. He said, "But they'll kill me if I don't pay them the money." It really doesn't matter Mr. Jenkins said, "Hey it doesn't matter if they parole you or put you behind bars, you're not going to get that money back. You'll have to work that problem out yourself. We deal with the law, do you understand?"

Jake just shook his head and sat quietly staring into space. Jenkins then said, "If we can convince them to parole you instead of locking you up, you'll have time to work that problem out in a few months."

Jake just looked at him. With a slight quiver in his voice he said, "Yeah, if I live that long."

"What did you say?" Jenkins asked.

"Nothing," Jake said, "nothing."

Jenkins got up and said, "I'll keep in touch and do the best I can. Good bye," and he left.

When Mr. Jenkins got back to his office, he had made a decision. He picked up the phone and called a private investigator who he hired for some of his cases. The investigator's name was Jordan Willis, a large, muscular man who was very good at his job.

"Hello," Jenkins said, "Jordan, I've got a job for you. There's a woman, Vickie Colden, who was married to a friend and client of mine. I want you to find out everything you can about her and I want you to dig as far back as you can into every little thing no matter how unimportant it might seem. I want it all. Can you get on it right away?"

"You've got it," Jordan said.

"I'll have my secretary mail you everything I have," Jenkins said. "You'll have it by tomorrow and he hung up."

CHAPTER 14

Mr. Jenkins sat at his desk pondering the situation. Then he picked up the phone and called the courthouse. A woman answered and said, "May I help you?"

"Yes," Jenkins replied, "is Judge Ryan in his chambers?"

The woman said, "I'll check. Who should I say is calling?"

"Dave Jenkins," he answered. "Tell him it's important."

"Please hold." There was a click and then Jenkins heard, "Hello, Dave, is that really you calling? I haven't talked to you for a long time; what are you up to?"

Jenkins answered, "Yeah, it's been a long time. I called to ask a favor. On Tuesday I'll be in your courtroom representing a young man named Jake Moran. The kid is a real mess. I'd really like to have you, if it's possible, release him into my custody. I'll be responsible for him."

"The name sounds familiar," the judge replied. "I'll look the case over and talk to you Tuesday morning when you get here."

Tuesday morning came soon enough. Jake was brought in the courtroom and sat down with Jenkins. The bailiff opened the door for the Judge and when Judge Ryan noticed Jenkins, he told the bailiff to bring Jenkins back to his chamber quickly. The judge went back to his chamber and waited for Jenkins. Soon, Dave Jenkins entered Judge Ryan's chamber.

"Dave," the judge said, looking at him sternly, "I've gone over the files on this boy. Do you know what you're asking me to do? That guy's got a rap sheet a mile long. If there ever was a true definition of a lost cause, he's it. What are you trying to do? Are you out of your mind? I can't do what you are asking. We'd both be crazy."

Jenkins walked around the front of his desk and then said, "You remember John Colden when we were in school? Well, he had two daughters. The oldest one just graduated from high school. She's so crazy about this guy you can't tell her anything bad about him, and if I keep tabs on him, the time will come when she sees him for what he is. That boy's had a rough time growing up. It's a miracle he's still alive."

Judge Ryan thought for a minute, and then asked him, "What if he gets out of hand and he gets into more trouble?"

Jenkins thought for a minute and said, "Then you can lock him up and throw away the key." Jenkins started walking to the door and as he started to open it, he turned and looked at the judge. "Give me one chance to save this girl from herself." Then he opened the door and went back into the courtroom and sat down by Jake.

Judge Ryan came into the court room, looked at Jake and said, "Jake Moran will you please approach the bench with your attorney?" Jake stood up along with Mr. Jenkins and they walked up to the bench. The Judge then looked at Jake and said, "I want you to look me straight in the eye and don't turn your head away. I want to make sure you see and hear everything I tell you."

The Judge was quiet for a few seconds, looking at Mr. Jenkins then back to Jake. Finally he said to Jake, "Son, I'm going to send you to an honor camp for one year. If you can behave yourself, I might shorten your time, and then I'm going to parole you to the custody of your attorney, for two more years. If you give this man any problems, I'll send you to the rock pile, do you understand me?"

"Yes sir," Jake replied in shock. Jenkins thanked the Judge for being lenient and left the courtroom; two officers took Jake back to his cell.

Jenkins got in his car and went back to his office. As he walked in the door his phone rang. His secretary answered and said, "It's for you, Dave."

He picked up his phone and said, "Hello." It was Amber wanting to know if he was able to help Jake. "I'm working on it," he said.

"Is he out of jail?" Amber asked.

"Well, no," Jenkins answered, "but I promised you I would help him."

"Oh, thank you," Amber said.

She started to hang up when Mr. Jenkins hollered, "Wait! I have to tell you something: Jake's probably going to spend a year in an Honor Camp. If he behaves, he might get out sooner. Do you understand; it's the best I could do." Amber's voice quivered and said, "Yes, goodbye," and hung up

School was out now, and Marsha was making her plans for college. Amber liked Marsha, for she had changed so much since she finally became her own person. But Amber's problem was bigger than Marsha's. Amber was a drug addict at the stage she would do anything to get them, and she was desperate with Jake gone.

Vickie was busy working the drug business and Paul was now working hard to get his prostitution business started.

Amber decided to look for a job. She went to department stores, grocery stores, travel places, beauty shops, looking for work, but found nothing. Jimbo hadn't been around for a while and she didn't know how to contact him.

Kim was busy with Rachel doing things around the church or at Rachel's house — anything so she didn't have to be around her step mother, Vickie.

One day when she was at Rachel's house Kim said, "I'm going to take a little walk. I've got things that I have to be alone to think about." She wandered out of the yard and around the corner, going up the street towards the cemetery. Walking past it she decided to go in and see her father's grave. She hadn't been back since he was buried and she felt like something was pulling her there. As she got close to the tomb stone, she began to shake and the tears started welling up in her eyes. She knelt down and started crying silently, saying in a shaky voice, "Daddy, why did you leave us? We need you, we need you; you don't know how much we need you. Things are so terrible right now. Vickie's on drugs, Amber is messing round with drugs, and she's got a boyfriend who's on drugs. She's a mess. We need you."

Finally she quit crying and was silent for a minute. Then she said with a slight smile, "I've got a new friend. Her name is Rachel. I like her very much. She's the best friend I've ever had. Her mom and dad are really nice people too. Her dad is the Pastor of the church about a block and a half from our house. You know the one. Rachel has taught me a lot about God. If she's right, we will see each other again someday. I'm not really sure yet if I want to believe that God is real, but it's better than doing drugs to bury your problems. I know that for a fact just by looking at what's going on around me, especially in school. But I've got the whole summer now just to be away from it all I hope. Well I guess I better go. I hope you'll do well wherever you're at." Kim stood up slowly and looked around to see if anyone was watching her and then walked away aimlessly not knowing where she was going.

Amber continued looking for a job, and she knew if she didn't find one she was going to have to deal with Vickie. In the downtown area, any place she saw a help wanted sign, she went in and filled out an application and was interviewed, but her mind was scrambled and she was discredited because of her strong overriding craving for drugs. It was so evident when she had an interview that something was wrong and she didn't make much sense when she talked or answered questions.

As she walked down the street, all of a sudden a car pulled over to the curb close to her and stopped. It was Paul. He got out, walked around the car to Amber. Paul was bound and determined to get Amber to work for him in his new venture, prostitution. She was quite pretty and very well put together. He also had personal desires of his own towards Amber.

"What do you want?" Amber said in disgust. "Just get out of here and leave me alone." She turned to walk away from him.

He reached out and grabbed her by the arm and stopped her. "Now don't run away from me. You need a job and I got a good proposition for you. You can really make some money working for me."

"Doing what?" Amber asked.

"Well," Paul said slowly. "I'm starting a sort of entertainment business for the elite businessmen in the town. I need pretty girls to entertain them in the evenings and nights."

"OK, you mean you want me to be a prostitute," Amber said as she tried to pull away.

"All right," Paul said keeping hold of her. "You are not so high above it. I know all about you. You've got a boy friend in jail and you got a drug problem. It takes money for that, and you can make it working for me, you can live high class."

"Let go of me," Amber yelled, getting angrier.

About that time a patrol car was driving by. The policeman saw Paul holding Amber and he slowed down to a crawl as he watched them. Paul saw him and released Amber, quickly got in his car and drove off. He couldn't afford any more attention from the law because of all the trouble he'd been in before.

The policeman stopped and looked at Amber. She looked at him, smiled, and walked on down the street as the officer drove on. Amber finally ended up back home. As she entered the house, she saw Vickie sitting at the table, drinking as usual. As she walked in, she turned to Vickie and said, "Your friend Paul stopped me on the street on my way home from looking for a job. He's trying to make a prostitute out of me."

"You stay away from him," Vickie yelled in anger. "Do you hear me?" She felt like she could kill Paul, but she cared for him too much so she just drank more, not knowing what to do.

Amber just laid on her bed thinking about Jake; she wasn't going to able to see him for a long time.

CHAPTER 15

Kim finally ended up at Rachel's house to see what she was doing. Rachel was in the back yard, working in the garden she had planted with a variety of vegetables. "Hi," Kim said as she walked thru the gate into the garden. "Need any help?" Kim asked as she fiddled with the buttons on her blouse.

"Sure," Rachel replied, "grab that little hand shovel and we'll plant some tomato plants over here." She pointed and walked to the spot.

"Boy, things are sure boring since schools been out, isn't it?"

"Well, yeah, I guess," Rachel answered. "You just got to find something you like to do and do it."

"Yeah," Kim replied. "Trouble is I don't know what I like to do."

Rachel looked at her, smiled, and said, "Well you like to sing and you're very good."

"Yeah, but that's only a couple of nights a week at practice," Kim replied.

"You're right," Rachel responded, "you need something else to do. Hey!" Rachel called to Kim, "do you want to go down to the deli shop and get something to drink? I'm buying.

"Sure," Kim replied.

They were approaching the deli when they heard a horn honk. It was Jeff. He pulled over to the curb. "You girls want to go for a ride?" he yelled.

"Yes," Kim said.

"No," Rachel replied at the same time. They looked at each other and then both said no, Kim knew that Rachel's mom would not like it. They were very protective of their daughter.

"You can come in and have a soda with us," Rachel invited.

"OK," Jeff responded and parked his car.

They all went in, found a booth, and sat down. The waiter came and took their orders. Jeff looked at Kim and said, "I haven't seen you for a couple of days — where have you been?"

"What do you mean, where have I been? You're the one who disappears!"

Jeff smiled, but did not answer. Then he said to Kim, "Hey, you know Tony, he's a friend of mine we kind of run together. We're thinking about having a camp out next Saturday night down by the lake. You know — we'll build a fire, roast some hot dogs and marshmallows and take some cold drinks along."

"You mean all night?" Kim asked with a serious look.

Jeff noticed the look on her face and said, "Well maybe, I don't know... it depends on how things go, you know, the weather and all that stuff."

Kim studied his face and sipped her drink, wondering what all that stuff meant. Her father had taught her some good moral standards, and she wasn't ready to throw them to the wind like her sister did. She could see the mess her sister was in and she did not want to end up like her.

"I don't know," Kim said. "I don't think I could stay out all night. My step-mother, you know." Kim didn't really have a clue what Vickie might say or do because of her life style of drugs, alcohol and mean disposition.

"Well, I'll talk to you about it later. I've got to go," he said as he got up and left. Rachel was kind of surprised he just got up and walked out like that, but Kim wasn't. She had seen some strange mood swings in his personality she didn't understand.

Meanwhile Jeff went cruising around town not really caring where he was going when he heard someone yell at him. He turned and looked; it was Jimmy, a sort of friend that hung around Jeff when he could. Jeff stopped and Jimmy ran to his car, out of breath, and asked, "where you going?"

"I don't know," Jeff said. "I've just been cruising around."

Jimmy was a short and skinny boy who dyed his hair three different colors. It was very evident he was on drugs most of the time because his speech and his eyes indicated he was in la-la land most of the time. He liked Jeff a lot and always tried to be his friend. Jeff allowed Jimmy to hang around with him sometimes, but not on a steady basis because he would get on your nerves talking about his girl and her problems. He was always crying on Jeff's shoulder and Jeff had enough problems of his own which he shared with no one.

Jeff arrived at home got out of his car and went in the house. He saw his mother standing in the kitchen watching him with a hard look on her face. "Where's my diamond bracelet?" she asked angrily.

"How would I know?" Jeff retorted.

"Don't give me that," she said, raising her voice angrily. "It was in my jewelry box on my dresser, so where is it? Did you sell it for drug money?

"Hell no!" Jeff responded. "You know I don't do drugs. Why do you always accuse me of using drugs?"

His mother was quiet for a moment. She said, "You know I lost your father because I believed you, because I was on your side. He kept trying to tell me you were into drugs because every valuable thing he had, including his coin collection, kept disappearing a little at a time. It's been hard raising you without him. If I had only listened to him he might still be here, but NO! I believed you. Now all my things are disappearing. My bracelet is gone, last month my diamond ring your father gave me on our anniversary, before that my earrings. I know now he was right and you're a liar."

"You don't know what you're talking about," he told her. He left the house, got in his car and drove away. His mother walked around the house crying, not knowing what to do.

Then she decided to call up her ex-husband, Jeff's father. She nervously dialed his number. It rang a long time and then a man answered.

"Is this Darren?" she asked.

"Yes," he replied. "Is that you, Sophie?"

"Yes," she replied through her tears.

"Are you all right?" he asked.

"No," she said, "I just wanted you to know I love you." She broke down and cried uncontrollably for she could hardly talk. "I'm sorry I didn't believe you. If only I would have listened to you," she cried. "Jeff is completely out of control. He steals anything of value he can get his hands on for drugs. I'm locking up everything that has personal value to me. Oh, Darren, I'm so sorry. I know you'll probably never come back, so just tell me what to do," she cried.

Darren was quiet for a minute and then said, "Look, my boss is sending me out of town for a week or so to check out some problems we're having at one of the stores. I'll call you when I get back and we'll go from there, ok?"

"Ok," she answered and hung up.

Jeff was cruising around the ice cream shop when he saw Jimmie leaning against the building smoking a cigarette. He pulled over and rolled the window down and yelled. "Jimmie, you want to go for a ride?"

"Sure." He jumped in the car.

Neither one said anything as they drove away. Jeff noticed that Jimmie just sat looking down very depressed. "What's up?" Jeff asked.

"Oh, it's my girl... she's mad at me and won't talk to me unless I promise to quit doing drugs and dying my hair. I could probably quit dying my hair if I wanted to, but I've tried to quit the drugs before and I just can't do it. I can't be without them; I'd go crazy, especially if I couldn't get any coke."

"She's just bluffing you," Jeff said. "She does drugs now and then herself."

"Yeah, but she just smokes pot," Jimmie responded. "I just know she doesn't do the hard stuff like you and me."

Jeff spoke up and told Jimmie, "Just let her go; find another girl."

"I don't want another girl," Jimmie replied. "I just want her. I'm crazy about her." Finally Jimmie asked Jeff to pull over and let him out.

Jeff pulled over and stopped. This time Jeff didn't know what to say, so he just kept quiet.

"I don't know what I'd do if I lost her." The tears started running down Jimmie's cheeks as he repeated in a low voice, "I don't know what I'd do." He turned with his head bent down and walked away. Jeff just shook his head, started his car and drove away.

CHAPTER 16

A week passed by and Amber was still trying to find a job without much success. Her dependence on drugs kept her pretty screwed up. As she was coming out of a store, walking through the parking lot, Jimbo called to her. She ran towards his car.

"Hi," he said with a big smile on his face, for he really liked Amber as a friend and maybe secretly a little more than that. Even though she was his best friend, Jake's, girl friend, he couldn't help but have a crush on her because she was very pretty and nice to him; girls never ever paid attention to him or were very nice to him like Amber.

"You want to go for a ride?" he asked.

"Oh, I don't know," she said shrugging her shoulders. "I guess we could just drive around."

As they drove aimlessly they talked about how much they missed Jake who was in an Honor Camp up state. Finally Amber nervously said to Jimbo, "Jimbo, I don't have any money. I'm trying to find a job, but I'm not having much luck." As she shuffled nervously looking at him, she finally said, "I sure need some coke. I'll pay you when I get a job."

Jimbo glanced at her as he drove and told her, "I've got a job, but I don't make much money. I'm working in a car wash four days a week, ten hours a day, but I just don't make much money. I'll give you a little bit, that's all I can afford," he said in a sad voice. As he handed it to her, she thanked him over and over. She couldn't wait for him to get someplace where no one would see them so she could satisfy her addiction; she hadn't had any for such a long time she was about to go out of her mind.

Jimbo also sniffed some coke and then he said, "I don't know when I'll be able to give you anymore. I just can't afford it."

"I know," Amber said, "I know."

After they finished, Jimbo drove her home and dropped her off. The next day Amber was on the prowl looking for a job. Her desperation for drugs was consuming her every thought when she saw Paul again. He pulled up to the curb and parked.

"Hello," he said with a big smile on his face. This time he took a different approach with her. "Look," he said, "I know how you feel and I understand, you got to have what you can't do without. Why suffer when there's an easy way to get it. You're a pretty girl. Take advantage of it: use it to get what, you want. You can make a lot of money. I promise you, a lot of money."

Amber didn't run this time. She just stood listening to him, staring at him, her mind churning. She was desperate and was getting more desperate by the minute. "What would I have to do?" she asked.

Paul saw how desperate she was, but he played cool so he wouldn't scare her away. "Well," he replied, "now I don't want to rush you. When you are ready, you call me and we will talk about it." He handed her a piece of paper with a phone number on it.

As Paul started to pull away, she said, "Wait," and she opened the door and got in. As they drove away, Paul said nothing. He was excited over getting her in his car. As they rode along, she finally asked, "What am I going to have to do?"

Paul thought for a minute and said, "You'll be an entertainer, showing men how to have a good time. Some like to drink and play games, some like to dance, some like to make out and some like to gamble. And if they want to have sex, well that's part of the entertainment, so you're not really a prostitute, just an entertainer."

Amber wasn't stupid. She knew that the word entertainer is just a cover word for a whore, but she didn't debate the issue with him. "How much can I make?" she asked.

"That's up to you," he replied. "If you work a few hours a night or more, it's up to you."

"Yeah, but how much will I make?" Amber asked again.

He thought for a moment and then explained to Amber. "You're a very pretty girl with a lot of sex appeal; you could make a hundred to two hundred dollars a night."

To Amber that sounded like a lot of money. She didn't realize for every hundred dollars she made, Paul would make two hundred. Amber needed money desperately to support her drug habit and at the moment, that was all there was. She nodded her head and said, "Ok, but don't you ever try to touch me, do you understand?"

"Ok," he said with a smile. "Fine with me." Then he said, "We'll have to get you some nice clothes. We can do that tomorrow."

"I've got clothes," Amber replied.

"But you need clothes designed for entertaining," he said. Amber knew exactly what he was talking about. She had seen prostitutes on the street before and she saw how they dressed.

Amber asked, "Can I have a small advancement?"

"What?" Paul said.

"I need money and I need it now."

"How much do you want?" he asked.

"Fifty dollars," she said.

Paul looked at her for a few seconds and said, "Ok, but if you skip out on me, you will be very sorry, do you understand me?"

"Yes," Amber replied, and he handed her the money. Paul pulled over and parked to let Amber out. She took off running looking for Jimbo, for she needed some cocaine bad.

That afternoon, Kim had gone home to do her chores. When she finished, she then went into the kitchen to see if Vickie would let her leave and go to Rachel's house. Vickie was passed out with her head laying on the table and a whiskey glass knocked over. Kim tiptoed out of the door and headed for Rachel's. When she got there, she knocked, and Rachel answered.

"Hi," Rachel said as Kim entered. Rachel's parents were having a discussion about a trip they were planning to take to visit another church about one hundred and fifty miles away. They had been invited by a man who had visited their church a while back and had been very impressed with Pastor Harding's teaching.

"I'm excited," Rachel said. "We're going on a trip. We haven't gone any place in a long time."

"How long are you going to be gone?" Kim asked.

"Oh, about a week to 10 days," Rachel said. "It'll be sort of like a vacation."

"Oh," Kim said with a long look on her face. She had become such close friends with Rachel. She didn't know what she would do while Rachel was gone.

Rachel noticed the look on Kim's face and asked "What's the matter?"

Kim was silent for a second and said, "Oh, I guess I'm going to miss you and your mom and dad. Ten days is a long time."

Rachel stared at Kim a minute and then went and whispered in her mother's ear. Then her mother went and whispered her father's ear.

He looked at Kim and then back at Rachel and nodded. Rachel became excited and ran back to Kim and said, "Why don't you come with us? You're more than welcome and we'll have fun."

Kim got excited — but what would Vickie say? That would be her biggest hurdle. Kim said, "I'll have to let you know." As she turned and was walking toward the door, she turned back and said, "I really want to go. See you later," and left.

Kim ran home, up the steps, and into the house, out of breath. She walked into the kitchen where Vickie was now awake, sipping on a drink. Kim walked up to the table and said, "I've done the things you wanted and I just wondered if there is anything else you wanted me to do."

Vickie looked at her a little puzzled and said, "Since when did you ever care what I wanted? You must want something," she mumbled.

"Well," Kim said slowly, looking down at the floor, "Rachel and her mom and dad are going on a week vacation and invited me to go along and I would like to go."

Vickie took a puff of her cigarette, then took a drink and then looked at her with a blank look. Then she looked away and said, "I don't give a damn if you want to go, just get the hell out of here. I've got enough problems to worry about now. You'll be just one less problem for a week," and then she took another drink. "Thank you," Kim responded, and then ran out the door. As she ran towards Rachel's house, she thought about what was said. She realized it was the first time she ever thanked Vickie for anything.

Kim knocked on the back door and Rachel answered. As she opened the door, Kim giggled and then shouted, "I can go, I can go!" They grabbed each other's hands and jumped up and down with joy. They immediately started making plans of what clothes they would take and other things they might want.

The next day Amber went to the store where Paul told her to go, and they would outfit her with a new wardrobe. Trying different things on she remarked, "Boy, That stuff is sure skimpy... it doesn't cover much."

When she came out of the store, she saw Paul waiting in his car. He got out and called to her, "Come on, get in. I want to show you something." She slowly walked toward his car and then got in. She loathed him so much she could hardly stand to be in the same car with him.

They drove to the edge of town where there were a lot of large homes, built seventy-five years ago. Then they parked in front of a three story house with ten bedrooms. It was an old but well kept house. "This is where we will do our entertaining," Paul said with a chuckle.

Amber didn't say anything. They went in and, Amber was amazed at how luxurious it looked. It was furnished with very expensive furniture. Wow, she thought to herself.

"Do you like it?" Paul asked. Amber just shrugged her shoulders and walked around looking in all the rooms downstairs. She wasn't interested in going upstairs. She already knew what the upstairs was for. She finally walked back outside to the car. Paul followed.

As they were driving away, Amber asked, "Why did you bring me out here?"

Paul replied, "I just wanted you to see that it is a very elite business. Not a dirty nasty thing, but a clean and good way of making money while satisfying others." Amber just looked at him very hard. In her mind, just because the place is high class, the people that use it are not. She thought, most of the men who came, whether they're wealthy or not, are just cheating on their wives or their girl friend. Who does he think he's kidding? But Amber also knew that she needed money. Jake was gone, for who knows how long, her drug addiction was expensive and she had to make lots of money to support it since she couldn't be without it. So, it was something she'd have to do for now, to keep from going out of her mind.

Within a block of Amber's house Paul pulled over to the curb. He told Amber she could walk home from there. Amber got out and started walking home. She knew he did that because he didn't want Vickie to see her in his car. He was having enough trouble with her now because of her jealousy over Amber. What Amber didn't know was the high profile distribution of drugs that Paul and Vickie were partners in. She just thought he was Vickie's boyfriend who could not be trusted.

Driving away, Paul still had his mind on Amber. He had a strong sexual lust for her, and it was getting stronger all the time. None the less, Paul had to be careful because of the prostitution business he was developing along with his other business in drugs. Thinking about it he soon realized the real purpose was to get Amber in bed without Vickie finding out. He smiled to himself as he thought about it and made plans.

Amber reached home and went in. Vickie was in her usual chair, drinking and smoking. She was a chain smoker. She was never without cigarette. Then Vickie hollered to Amber, "Your sister is going to be gone for a week, so you can do some of her chores," and got up from her chair and went into her bedroom.

CHAPTER 17

It was Friday morning and Kim was at Rachel's door with her suitcase packed and her handbag. Beverly answered the door and there Kim stood gleaming from ear to ear. "I'm ready to go," Kim said excitedly.

"You sure are," Beverly responded with a big smile.

Rachel came to the door and grabbed Kim's suitcase and said, "Come to my room, I'm not finished packing."

Beverly looked at her husband and said, "Boy, talk about two excited girls!" He just smiled and went about getting ready for their trip too. They got everything loaded into their Suburban and in no time at all they were on their way.

The two hour trip was finally over as they reached Green River. As they drove around reading and following the maps, they finally found the church they were looking for without any problems. Pastor Harding got out of his car and went into the church office, while his wife and the girls waited in the car.

In the office, the secretary looked up and asked, "May I help you?"

"I'm Pastor Harding and I'm here to meet with Elder John Costa."

"Oh yes," she said, "we've been expecting you. Follow me." They went back outside, she pointed down the street and said, "Just drive down to the next block and as you cross the side street, it's the second house on the left, the very large two story white house."

"Thank you very much," Pastor Harding said. He then drove down the street, pulled into the driveway, and parked. They all walked up to the door and rang the bell. Mrs. Costa answered the door.

"I'm Pastor Harding," he began but before he had a chance to introduce himself and family Mrs. Costa said excitedly, "Oh, we've been expecting you. My husband isn't home from work yet but he'll be here soon." She was very excited as she helped bring their suitcases and other things in the house. They went upstairs and she showed the girls their room.

"When you get unpacked, come downstairs. I'll have dinner on the table because John will be home any minute."

John came in through the door as they were coming down the stairs. As he saw them, a broad smile covered his face. He shook Jim & Beverly's hands and welcomed the girls. Mrs. Costa was directing everyone where to sit when their son Mike, walked in the door and straight to the table.

"Hi," he said as he went to his chair.

"Just a minute young man," his mother said, "I want you to meet Pastor Harding and his wife Beverly, and this is Kim and Rachel."

"Hello," he said looking at the girls. His eyes were focused on Kim. She was about the prettiest girl he'd ever seen. He was totally captivated, staring at her. Kim was embarrassed.

His mother said, "You can sit down now, Mike."

"Oh," he said, embarrassed, and sat down.

While Jim and John discussed church business after dinner, their wives and the girls went into the living room to talk. Mike went upstairs to clean up and change his clothes. When he came down he went to where the women were. He stood listening to them talk for a few minutes and then joined in.

"There's a dance at the church hall tonight and there will be refreshments and stuff. Well, I kind of wondered if you girls would like to go."

"Yes!" Kim said and then looked at Rachel. Rachel looked at her mom, because back at their church, dancing wasn't allowed.

Beverly looked at Rachel, then got up and said, "Excuse me for just a minute." She walked into the other room where the men were talking. She whispered in Pastor Harding's ear. He answered her and then continued his discussion with Mr. Costa. Beverly went back to the girls and sat down. She looked at Rachel and said, "I think it will be all right."

The girls were excited. "Ok," Mike said, "I'll call you when it's time to go." His eyes were still on Kim as he left the room.

While Mrs. Harding and Mrs. Costa chatted, Kim and Rachel went to another part of the room. "I don't know how to dance," Rachel said.

"Oh it's easy," Kim responded, "you'll catch on fast." Time past slowly for the girls as they waited for Mike. They went upstairs and got dressed for the occasion. They put on their very best dresses and as they came down the stairs, Mike showed up.

He looked at them kind of puzzled. He sort of stuttered and then finally said, "This isn't a dress up kind of dance. You can wear the Levis you had on. That'll be just fine."

They ran back upstairs, into their room and changed clothes again the came back downstairs.

Mike said, "Yeah, that's great. You guys look good." They said good-by and left.

At the church hall Mike introduced them to the other teenagers who came up to them. Finally the band started playing. It was made up of some of the boys and girls who went to the church. Immediately, Mike asked Kim to dance.

Rachel stood around watching the kids dance and watched their footwork so she could learn. Then a boy approached her and said, "Hi, my name is Donnie, what is yours?"

Rachel was feeling very warm but her hands were cold and sweaty and her face flushed. "Rachel," she said. This was the first time any boy had ever approached her and she wasn't sure how to act. Rachel noticed he was cute and a little shy.

"Would you like to dance?" he said, not too sure of himself.

"I don't know how to dance," Rachel replied, a little embarrassed.

"Oh that's ok," he said. "I'm not very good myself. Maybe we can sort of learn together."

"Well, ok," Rachel responded and walked out on the floor with him. They danced slowly, trying to catch on. Rachel said, "Our church doesn't allow dancing," Rachel said. "They say it's a sin." "They used to be like that, too," Donnie answered. "But we know now, since reading more of the Bible, people danced for joy. They finally woke up." Rachel was enjoying herself with a boy, for the first time in her life and she couldn't remember having so much fun.

Meanwhile, back in Clement City, Jeff was cruising around town and not knowing what to do with himself. He had been looking for Kim. She never told him she was leaving for a week. In her excitement, she just forgot.

As he cruised by the parking lot of a big shopping mall where some of the guys hung around, he saw a boy he recognized from school, running towards his car waving his arms, so he stopped and rolled his window down. "Jeff," the boy yelled, "you better come over here quick; your friend Jimmie's gone crazy. He's got a gun."

Jeff parked his car and followed him to where about a dozen guys were doing drugs and smoking pot. They were all teasing Jimmie because he was crying and yelling he was going to kill himself. "Go ahead," one boy laughed, half stoned out of his head from the drugs.

"Shut up!" Jeff yelled at the guy.

Then Jeff walked slowly up to Jimmie. Jimmie just looked at him with tears running down his cheeks and a sawed off shotgun in his hands. "Where in the world did you get that gun?" Jeff asked.

"A guy gave it to me for the money he owed me for drugs... a couple of months ago. I've had it hid in my closet in case I ever needed a gun," he said, choking back the tears.

"Why are you doing this, Jimmie?" Jeff asked, as calmly as he could, trying to calm Jimmie down. As the tears flowed, Jeff was wondering what kind of drugs he was on. Jimmie was so upset, Jeff couldn't tell.

"My girl broke up with me," Jimmie cried. "She said she didn't want anything to do with me anymore and that she had another boy friend. I can't live without her," Jimmie cried. "She's the only one that ever cared about me and treated me good. I love her so much. My parents don't give a damn about me. I don't have anybody now."

"I'm still your friend," Jeff said, pleading.

"That's not the same," he repeated.

Jeff pleaded, "Come take a ride with me and we'll get away and we'll get everything worked out, ok?"

"No!" Jimmie yelled. "No, I don't want to ride with you. Just go away and leave me alone."

Jeff realized he wasn't helping, only making things worse. "Ok," Jeff said in a quiet voice. "I'll tell you what... I'll go back to my car and wait for you. When you're feeling better, come on over, and we'll go for a ride."

"Just go away," Jimmie said in a much calmer voice.

Jeff smiled and responded, "I'll wait for you," and he turned and walked away.

He had only taken about fifteen steps when he heard a loud blast. He turned around quickly.

Jimmie had put the barrel under his chin and pulled the trigger. The blast blew his head to pieces.

Then one of the boys yelled, "Let's get the hell out of here," and they ran in all directions.

Jeff ran back to Jimmie. "Jimmie, why, why?" Jeff knelt down and just held him, rocking back and forth and crying, "Why? Why?"

Then he could hear sirens way off in the distance getting louder and louder until the police arrived. Two officers pulled Jeff loose from Jimmie's body. Jeff was crying uncontrollably as a policeman tried to question him. The officer kept asking him who the kid was and where he got the gun. But Jeff couldn't talk. He just kept shaking his head and saying, "Why? Why? Why?"

An ambulance finally came and they picked up Jimmie's body and took it away. The police took Jeff to the station and called his mother. Jeff was just sitting in the chair staring into space when she arrived. She looked around and finally saw him.

As she rushed to him, an officer stopped her, wanting to know who she was. "I'm his mother," she said, and he let her go. She put her hands on Jeff's shoulders and bent down. Very softly she asked, "What happened?"

Jeff slowly turned his head and said, "Jimmie blew his brains out, that's what happened," as the tears started to flow again. He paused a bit, and then went on, "Over a girl, Mom, over a girl!"

A policeman came up then and told her, "You can take your son home, Mrs. Miller. His car is still in the parking lot at the mall. You can take him there so he can pick it up," and he walked away. Jeff got up, and he and his mother left.

Meanwhile, back at the dance in Green River, Kim and Rachel were enjoying themselves. It was getting late and the dance was almost over. Rachel was introducing Kim to Donnie when Mike approached them. "Well, its time to go," he said with a smile. "All good things must come to an end, unfortunately." Mike looked at Donnie and asked, "Have you got a ride home?"

"No," Donnie said, "it's not so far, I can walk."

Mike looked at Rachel then looked back at Donnie and said, "No you can come with us. We'll give you a ride. No point in walking if you don't have to." They all got in the car and drove away. In the car they started making plans for what they could do the rest of the week.

"We could go swimming out at the lake," Mike suggested.

The two girls agree, that would be fun, too. "Then," Mike continued, "we could go to a Carnival over in Wilsonville the next day." The girls liked that as well. They all decided to go to a movie also.

The days passed quickly and Kim couldn't remember the last time she had so much fun, or if ever. She just wished it could never end.

Pastor Harding and Elder Costa had pretty much concluded their business. Pastor had agreed after talking to his wife that he would take the position as Pastor of the Church in Green River. When the news was shared with Rachel she was very excited because she was beginning to like Donnie very much and she never had a boyfriend before. But then, as Rachel thought about it more, she was very sad because she had come to love Kim like a sister, so much that she had very mixed emotions. Kim felt sad as well because she didn't know if she would see Rachel anymore. Kim was also beginning to like Mike very much as well, even though she still had feelings toward Jeff back home.

The week was about over and everyone was saying good-bye. The car was all packed. Walking to the car, Mike reached out and pulled Kim aside. "I don't quite know how to say this, but it really has been fun with you and I want you to know, I'm really going to miss you. I never met anyone like you before. You are so beautiful, inside and out; I really hope with God's help I'll see you again." Kim looked at him for a moment thinking, what a gentleman he is. She told him she would miss him too. She had never met a boy before that talked and treated her like a lady and she enjoyed it very much. Then they all said good-bye and Mike grabbed Kim and gave her a great big hug. He really didn't want her to go.

On the drive home Rachel asked, "When will we be moving?"

"Not for a few months," her father said. "They have to find a replacement for me." The girls sat in the back seat and talked about all the things they had never done before like going dancing, swimming in a lake, going to a carnival, and to the movies. The other thing that amazed them is they never saw any drug activity going on or anyone who even looked like they were on drugs.

CHAPTER 18

As they were heading home and the excitement wore off, Kim fell asleep. Rachel was getting tired also, but she had something on her mind. She tapped her mother on the shoulder, leaned forward and asked, "Mom, back home in school last year, I heard some girls talk about the dances they had gone to and all the different drugs they could get there. We didn't see any drugs at the dance in Green River or anything that looked suspicious as far as drugs are concerned. I don't understand how two towns could be so different!"

Her mother thought for a minute. "Well you have to remember that was probably all Christian kids at the dance. They all go to church together so their attitude on drugs is a lot different than what the kids on the street or in public schools would think. You're blessed because you have someone to believe in and an example to follow. In the country we live in today, most kids don't get much parental input about what's right and wrong or what's good or bad. The reason is because in most families, the father and mother both work in order to make ends meet financially, so most children are on their own and follow the popular or easiest way to live, according to the world around them. You can't imagine what you might get into when you don't get any guidance or truth." Rachel thought for a second and said, "Wow, that makes sense! Thanks, mom." Then she sat back and went to sleep.

They finally reached home and went by Kim's house and let her out first, then went on home.

It was early afternoon as Kim walked in the door. Vickie was in her chair in the kitchen as usual, drinking and smoking a cigarette. "Well," Vickie slobbered, as Kim walked in. "I'll bet you hated to come home, huh?"

Kim didn't answer. She just said, "I need to put my stuff away."

"Did you know a kid named Jimmie?" Vickie asked as Kim turned to go to her bedroom.

She stopped, looked back at Vickie and said, "Yeah, kind of. He hung around Jeff now and then."

"Yeah," Vickie said, "that's the kid. It was in the paper. He blew his damn brains out with a shotgun. They said it was over a girl. Imagine," Vickie said, "He blew his brains out for a girl. What an idiot." She chuckled as she took another drink. Kim was stunned. She wondered how Jeff was. Maybe she ought to try to find him.

Then she remembered, she had his phone number. She asked Vickie, "Can I leave for a while? I would like to find Jeff."

Vickie who was pretty numb from drinking, nodded her head, and made a gesture with her hand as if to say, get out of here.

Kim headed for the malt shop to use a pay phone. She didn't want to talk to Jeff in front of Vickie. She called his home and his mother answered. "Is Jeff home?" Kim asked.

"No," she said. "I don't know where he is. He's really shook up right now over what's happened. He might be out just cruising or with some other friends."

"Thank you," Kim said and hurried off.

Amber was at the big house for her first day of work. After changing clothes, she was assigned to where she would be working, with an older woman who was in charge. Amber had never seen her before. She just knew that she was the boss. Her name was Bertha and that's all she went by. Amber walked out of the room. She heard other female voices down stairs. She walked quietly down the stairs to see what some of the others looked like. As she reached the bottom, she saw about six young women talking to Bertha about what they were supposed to do. Amber noticed that they were all older than her except for one whom she recognized immediately. It was Rosie from school. It didn't surprise her though, knowing Rosie's reputation at school.

Rosie spotted Amber, "Well, hello," she said in a sarcastic tone. "So you are going to be working here too — well, well."

Amber didn't answer. She just went back up the stairs to her room wishing the night would never come. Soon she heard steps of someone coming to her door. They knocked and Amber opened it very slowly. When the door was fully opened, there stood Paul. She was a little scared at first as he said to her, "Come on downstairs; I want to show you something. He took her into a very large room, which she had seen before. But now it had a bar in one corner and lots of tables and chairs.

"This is where you'll work," he told her. "The room is for playing cards, eating, drinking and gambling. You'll serve drinks and food. Bertha will teach you how to mix drinks. That ought to make you happy," he said. "You won't have to go to bed with anybody. That won't make you the kind of money you would make otherwise, but I'll pay you good. You'll get by all right."

Amber was happy, very happy. She went over in her mind everything Paul had just said to her and hoped she could make it. She also thought maybe Paul wasn't as bad as she thought. He was being very sensitive toward her. What she didn't know is that Paul gave her the job because he wanted to keep her for himself when the time was right.

"We're going to be open for business starting this week end." He looked at Bertha and told her, "You've got a lot to teach her, so you better get busy."

"You bet," Bertha said. She took Amber with her as Paul left.

Amber got home late. When she went in and closed the door, she woke Vickie up who was asleep with her head lying on the table next to her drink. "I got a job," Amber said.

"What kind of a job?" Vickie mumbled.

"I'm a waitress in a night club," Amber said. "I have to work late hours."

Vickie just looked at her and laid her head back down. Kim was already asleep when Amber went in the room so she quietly slipped into bed.

Morning came and Kim was up at the crack of dawn. She went in the kitchen and started cleaning up the mess Vickie usually left, such as liquor spills on the counter, table and floor. Cigarette butts were all over the place along with dirty dishes. When she finished, Amber and Vickie were still asleep so she went out the back and fed Molly, her little dog and played with her for a while. Then she walked around the house to the front yard.

As she came around the corner of her house, she was shocked to see Jeff just sitting in his car, scooted down in the seat, sleeping. She walked up and knocked on the window but he didn't move. She pounded harder and he finally woke up. He scooted up and rolled the window down.

"What are you doing here?" she asked with a smile.

He rubbed his eyes trying to wake up. He said, "I've been driving around all night. Sometimes I would just park wherever I was and sleep. I don't even remember coming here."

"When did you get home?" Jeff asked.

"Yesterday", Kim answered.

"I heard what happened to your friend when I got back," said Kim. "Are you alright?"

"Yeah, I guess," Jeff replied, staring into space. Then he shook his head and said, "It was stupid, just stupid... over a damn girl."

Kim didn't say anything in return, for she knew what it felt like to lose someone like she lost her father. It didn't make any sense. What she didn't realize was that Jimmie was all screwed up mentally on drugs.

"Do you want to go for a ride?" Jeff asked.

"Sure," said Kim and got in the car.

As they drove away he asked her, "Did you have fun while you were gone?" "Yes," Kim replied. "I danced for the first time in a long time, went swimming in a lake, and went to a carnival. I had lots of fun."

"Sounds like it," he said. "Are you hungry?

"Yes," Kim responded.

I'm broke," Jeff said. "Let's go to my house and I'll get my mom to feed us." Jeff's mother had just been up long enough to get dressed when they got there. As they walked in Jeff just glanced at her and said, "Mom, This is Kim. Would you fix us something to eat?" His mother hesitated for a few seconds and said, "Sure," and headed for the kitchen.

Jeff told Kim, "I'll be back in a minute," and headed for the bathroom.

Kim quietly went in the kitchen and sat down at the table. Jeff's mother watched her as she started cooking. "How does bacon and eggs sound?" she asked Kim.

"Very good," Kim answered.

"Are you the same girl I've talked to on the phone?" she asked.

"Yes,"

"You're a pretty girl," she said as she kept looking at Kim.

"Thank you," Kim answered again.

Jeff finally came in the kitchen and sat down. His mother served them and went into the other room. They finished eating and got up and went in the other room also.

"We'll see you," Jeff said and went out the door heading for his car. Kim stopped and turned to Jeff's mother. "Thank you so much for breakfast; it was really good." As she turned to go, Jeff's mother got up quickly and rushed to Kim and grabbed her arm.

"Kim, I'd like to talk to you alone sometime. I need your help with something. Can we meet sometime? I really would like to talk to you." Sure, Kim replied. I'll give you a call," and then left.

As she was getting in the car, Jeff asked, "What did she want from you?"

"Nothing," Kim responded. "She just asked if I could get together with her sometime and talk, that's all."

"Yeah," Jeff said. "I don't know what she'd want to talk about."

A few days passed as Kim kept wondering what Jeff's mom wanted to talk about. She didn't know her at all, so she was a little hesitant to call her. Finally Kim made the call and went over to Jeff's house. She stood in front of the door for a few seconds, wondering where Jeff was since his car wasn't there. She rang the doorbell and Sophie answered.

As Kim walked in she asked, "Where is Jeff?"

"I don't have any idea," she replied. "He told me yesterday that he wouldn't be home for a couple of days; he just wanted to be alone. That's why I had you come over today. Come sit at the table with me. I'll get us something to drink. What would you like?"

"Water is fine," Kim answered. Sophie went in the kitchen, got the drinks and came back. As she sat down, Kim noticed how tired and haggard she looked.

Sophie stared at Kim for a second and then said, "I really don't know where to start. You're the first girl I've ever seen Jeff sincere about. When he talks about you, it's with respect and very deep feelings. I think he's crazy about you. You are very pretty and I can tell you're a good girl by the things he says when he mentions you."

Then her voice broke as she was trying to hold the tears back.

"Kim, I'm afraid for Jeff and I'm hoping you can help me with him." Kim just sat quietly listening to her. Sophie continued, "I know Jeff is doing drugs and he's getting worse. He has stolen just about everything of value to me and sold them for money to pay for his drug problem. He gets a liberal allowance from his father even though his father doesn't have anything to do with him. His father knows he's doing drugs, but he's been gone a couple of years and doesn't know how bad it is now. Over the past three years I've seen his grades in school go from very high marks to where now he is barely passing. He lies all the time." Then the tears came. Sophie's tears were flowing and her voice quivered as she spoke.

"I went in his room a few days after my husband left and Jeff was laying on his bed, smoking something that looked like a cigarette. I asked him what it was as I bent over him because he was acting weird, and saw his eyes just rolling around and I realized he didn't even see me or know I was there." Her voice groaned, "Realizing that my husband was right, I was very stupid and naïve. It was just so hard to believe. We were good to Jeff. We did things together as a family. He had a good relationship with his father and me, I thought. All of a sudden he just started changing: his habits, the way he ate, the things he talked about, sometimes he didn't even make any sense. If my husband questioned him about different things he would go on the defensive and it used to never be like that. We used to be able to talk to him. He was such a good kid before he got into drugs. I love my son, but I'm at my wits end. I don't know what to do. I'm desperate. I'm afraid something bad might happen to him like his friend Jimmie. There is nothing left for him to steal, so I don't know what he'll do for money. I'm hoping that he cares for you enough that you would be able to influence him into getting help or trying to quit. The one thing I'm really worried about is that he may have been on them so long now that it's too late. I sincerely hope not. Will you help me?" she pleaded.

Kim looked down at the table and said, "I really like Jeff and I always knew something strange going on with him. Sometimes he would just disappear. When he got fidgety or nervous, I suspected he might be doing drugs, but I guess I didn't really want to believe it either. He's really sweet when he acts normal, but lately that's not very often."

Kim was quiet for a few seconds and then said, "You know, I don't do drugs and I never will. My sister's on them, and I see what it's doing to her. It scares me and I can't seem to talk to her about it. I'd better go," Kim said. "1 will really try to help."

CHAPTER 19

Kim walked down the street feeling pretty numb. Why does life have to be so complicated? She thought. Why do kids have to do drugs? Why do they have to kill themselves? Why? Why? The only true friend she has, that doesn't seem to have these problems is Rachel. What would she do if she didn't have a friend like her? She thought.

Before she knew it, she was at Rachel's house. She knocked on the door and Rachel answered it. They went to Rachel's room, sat on the bed and talked. Kim told her about her visit with Jeff's mother. Rachel listened intently. When Kim finished talking out her problems, she stood up and looked at Rachel. Then she said, "Is God real? Why doesn't he stop all This? Why does he allow it?"

Rachel looked up at her and said, "Because he gave us a free will. We have the right to go to heaven or hell, whatever way we choose. It's our choice."

Kim smiled and said, "I've got to go home and get my work done."

When she got home, she checked to see what she had to do in the kitchen. She looked at the slightly opened door to Vickie's bedroom and noticed Vickie out cold, lying on the bed with an empty glass still in her hand.

She then decided to go outside and check on Molly because she didn't hear her barking and whining like she usually did when she and Amber came home. As she opened the back door, she noticed Molly wasn't at the edge of the steps with her rope stretched as far as it would go. She looked in her little house and noticed she was just lying very still. Kim got scared and reached in and shook her. Molly didn't respond. Her body was limp. Kim started crying. She grabbed Molly, unsnapped her rope and ran around the house, not knowing what to do. Then she ran down the street to Rachel's. She kicked the door hard and Rachel's mother answered.

"Something is wrong with Molly," Kim cried. "I can't get her to wake up. What'll I do?"

Beverly grabbed her car keys and said, "Let's take her to the vet." They rushed and got in the car. Beverly hurried to the vet's office, which wasn't too far away. They rushed in the door.

"Somebody help us," Kim cried as the tears were still running down her cheeks. A nurse hurried them through door and led them to the emergency room. The vet came in and quickly started checking Molly all over.

He gave Beverly a look that meant something was really wrong. He checked her heart and then looked at them and said, "I'm sorry, but she's dead."

Kim screamed and grabbed Molly and hugged her tightly. Beverly and the doctor very gently pried her loose from the dog. She didn't want to let go. Kim sat down in a chair and sobbed. Beverly went up to the doctor and asked, "Could you find out what she died from?"

"Sure," he said. "I'll run some tests and then call you." The doctor asked, "What do you want me to do with the body?"

Before Beverly could answer, Kim spoke up through her tears. "We'll bury her with my Mom and Dad." The doctor looked at Beverly and nodded, yes they would bury her there. A few hours after Beverly and Kim had left and arrived back at Rachel's, the vet called and informed Beverly the dog had been poisoned. Beverly sat down with Kim and told her the sad news.

"She did it!" Kim screamed. "I know she did it. She hated Molly. I know she did it." Kim ran out the door and headed home before Beverly could stop her. She had never seen a look like that in Kim's eyes before. She never saw the anger in Kim like that and she was concerned about her.

Kim reached home, ran up the steps and hurried in the house looking for Vickie. Her anger was so strong it overcame her fear of Vickie. There was Vickie sitting in her usual spot drinking.

Kim hurried straight to the table in front of her, leaned forward and screamed, "You witch, you killed my dog!"

"Shut up," Vickie said. She took another drink.

"I'll get even with you," Kim said. "I don't know how or when, but I'll get even." Then she stormed out of the house.

Vickie just stared at the door. She was a little shook up. She had never seen that side of Kim before and it scared her a little. Kim headed for the park and sat down still crying. Then she laid her head down on the bench and cried herself to sleep.

Meanwhile Mr. Jenkins was just returning to his office. His secretary came in and gave him a message from Jordan Willis, the investigator whom he hired to check Vickie out. The message read that he may have some startling information on her, but he wanted to check some more on other leads he had. He was just keeping Jenkins up on what was happening. His last statement was this woman is a real loser. Jenkins just smiled and called the court house to talk to the judge, to let him know the information coming forth about Vickie will justify holding off the decision of John's will.

Evening was coming and Amber arrived at her job. She went in, straight to the bar and was getting things ready when the house mother, Bertha, walked in. Amber said, "I'm having trouble with the mixing of some of the drinks. Could you go over them again with me?"

"Sure," she said as she stepped behind the bar.

Bertha asked Amber, "What's your relationship with Paul?"

Amber said, "He's my step-mother's boyfriend."

"Is that all?"

Amber hesitated for a second and said, "Yes, I hope so."

Bertha said, "You be careful of him. You seem different then the other girls. So you watch out." That scared Amber a little, what did she mean by that statement? Paul promised to leave her alone. Now that uneasy feeling about him crept over her again.

It was late morning the next day. Jenkins sat at his desk going over some court cases coming up, when the phone rang. It was the investigator.

"I got some pretty good stuff on your Vickie. Listen to this," he said. "She's wanted in New York under the name of Vickie Chapman for Drug Trafficking. She disappeared before she could be arrested. I think she is also Vickie Wells that was being perused by the law in Chicago for drug trafficking, and I also think she's the same Vickie Chapman wanted for drug trafficking in Denver. She also had an accomplice, a man who fits the description of Paul Messer you told me about. She ran his operation pretty much the same way in all the other cities she's been in. Send me a picture of this Messer guy as soon as you can."

"1 will," Jenkins answered. "Thank you," he said and hung up. Jenkins pondered on how he would get these pictures for him. He wondered if maybe the girls could help him. He called their home and Vickie answered.

"This is Mr. Jenkins," he said. "I need to talk to Amber and Kim concerning the will of their father. Could you have them call me, please."

Vickie was quiet, then said, trying to sound nice and sweet, "All right, I'll tell them as soon as I see them. Amber has a good job and Kim spends a lot of time with her friends. I'll have them call you, goodbye."

Vickie slammed the phone down. When the hell is that will going to be settled? She wondered. This crap's gone on long enough. I wonder if he's up to something. Well, I was his wife and he ain't gonna screw me. I'll see to that. She sat down and poured herself another drink

A few hours later Kim came walking in the house. Vickie heard her and began yelling at her. "When you see your sister, give your attorney a call. He wants to talk to you."

"What did he want?" Kim asked in a sarcastic tone.

"How in the hell should I know," Vickie said, "just call him."

Kim went to the phone and called Mr. Jenkins. "Hello," she said, "this is Kim, Mr. Jenkins. You wanted to talk to me?"

"Yes," he said, "I need to talk to you and Amber as soon as I can. Now just answer yes or no, when I'm talking. Is Vickie there with you?"

"Yes," said Kim.

"She is not to know or suspect anything suspicious, do you understand?"

"Yes," Kim said.

"You talk to your sister and find a way you can meet me somewhere or call me when no one is around to know about it. We have to keep this secret. Do you understand me? Just tell Vickie that I will call and give you a time when I can have a meeting with you girls. If she asks what about tell her you don't have any idea."

"All right," Kim said. "Goodbye." Kim hung up.

"What in the hell does he want?" Vickie hollered.

"I don't have any idea," Kim said. "He just said he would call you when he could set up an appointment to talk to us." Then she turned and went into her room. She hated to be anywhere around Vickie.

Kim fought to stay awake that night so she could talk to Amber. It was two a.m. when Amber got home. Amber went in her room and started undressing when she heard Kim whisper as quietly as she could. "Amber, I got to talk to you, please."

Amber went over to Kim's bed and sat down. "What's up?" she whispered.

"Mr. Jenkins called," Kim said. "He wants to have a secret meeting or telephone conversation with us without anyone knowing about it."

"What for? Amber asked.

"I don't know," Kim said, "but it's got to be a secret. No one is to know, so let me know when you want to do it and I'll call him."

"Ok," Amber said, and she went to bed.

CHAPTER 20

Amber was making enough money now to support her drug habit, but now she wanted her own car to get around instead of walking or depending on Jimbo to take her places. She went to a used car lot looking to see what it would cost, since she had no idea. It was kind of a dumpy place at the lower end of town. As she roamed around the cars she happened to look up and was shocked to see Paul across the street. He was talking to the same two men she had seen talking to Jake in the old building across from the school. Amber was totally unaware that Paul and Vickie were in the drug business together. She knew Vickie used drugs heavily, but that was all. She didn't let Paul see her as she watched them; they talked for a long time. Then Paul got in his car and drove away, and the two men did the same. Amber finally found a little car she liked. Now, the big hurdle will be to convince Vickie to sign for her.

Amber finally reached home. As she walked in the door, she looked for Vickie. Vickie was just coming out of her bedroom. She seemed very calm and Amber judged that she had taken drugs to settle her down. "Can I talk to you for a minute?" Amber asked.

"Sure, what you want?" Vickie asked as she sat down at the kitchen table where she always sat.

"I got a good job now," Amber said, "and I would like to get a car, but you would have to sign for me."

"I'm not signing a damn thing," Vickie yelled. "Hell, I don't even have a car and you think I'm going to sign for you."

"Why don't you have a car?" Amber asked.

"Cause I don't want one," Vickie responded. The truth was Vickie had her license suspended in another state before she married John. She knew because of her addiction to drugs and alcohol, she could never drive again. Amber didn't push it. She decided to let it go for now. It was getting late in the afternoon, so she started getting ready for work.

It was about 9:00 pm when Paul arrived at the big house, and it was busy. He walked in, walked around to see how things were. Going into the game room he noticed Amber at the bar cleaning glasses. He always noticed Amber. As he walked up to her he said, "How are you, honey?"

"I'm not your honey," Amber responded.

Paul shrugged and said, "Sorry, what's the matter? You look down in the dumps."

Amber paused for a moment, then turned and looked at him. "I want to get a car so I don't have to depend on the bus or someone else to get me around, and Vickie won't sign for me."

"Is that all?" Paul said.

"Is that all!" Amber said. "That's enough!" Then she turned' her back to him and continued to clean glasses.

Paul thought for a moment and then said, "I'll sign for you, if it means that much to you."

Amber turned and looked at him, thinking what would Vickie say or do. She knew how jealous she was of Paul. She wondered what the consequences might be. But then she decided she didn't care. She wanted a car and she fell in love with the little car she found. She gave the man Fifty dollars to hold it until she could find a way to buy it. "All right," she said. "But no strings attached!"

"No strings attached," Paul said with a smile.

The next day Amber was driving down the street in her car. She was so excited she could hardly stand it. She headed over to Rachel's looking for Kim. The girls were out in the yard when they saw Amber drive up. Kim's eyes got real big as she looked in disbelief.

"You got a car," she yelled with a big smile.

"You're darn right," Amber said. "It's mine! You and I have to talk," Amber said as she looked at Rachel.

Rachel took the hint and said, "I'll be in the house," and she left.

"We've got to call Mr. Jenkins," Amber said, "but I'm afraid to try to do it at home. Do you think Rachel's parents would let us use their phone? We could use a pay phone but somebody might see us."

"I'll ask," said Kim. "Come on in."

Amber and Kim went to the door and knocked. Rachel answered. "Do you think your parents would let us use your phone?" Kim asked. "We have to call our attorney and we don't want to do it from home."

"It'll be all right," Rachel's mother answered as she overheard the conversation. "Lets' see," Mrs. Harding said as she led them to the pastor's private study. "Here you go — there are two phones in here on the same line. That will make it easier for you."

Mrs. Harding left, closing the door behind her. Kim dialed Mr. Jenkins office. His secretary answered and transferred the call to him. Putting the phone to his ear, he heard, "this is Kim, and

Amber is on the other phone. We're at the Pastor's house in his office and no one is here."

"Ok, girls," Mr. Jenkins said. "You know I've been hoping for a miracle and I think I've got one, concerning your father's Will. I hired an investigator to check up on Vickie and it seems she's had a lot of run-ins with the law, and I think she's still running under an assumed name. But we need more on that guy Paul. The biggest thing we need on him is a picture of him. I need your help to get it. He keeps a low profile."

Then Amber spoke up. "He comes in now and then where I work." She didn't want Mr. Jenkins to know she worked for Paul, or had anything to do with him and she didn't want him to know what kind of job she had.

"Good," Mr. Jenkins said. "What would be the best time to do it?"

"Late afternoon, before it gets dark," Amber said. "But how are you going to do it?"

"I'll have a man parked in a car a good distance who won't be noticed and just hope we can get a good shot," he said. "Let's try for tomorrow after-noon. Will that work for you?" he asked.

"Sure," Amber said. "I'll get him out there somehow."

"Ok," he said, "and good luck."

The next day came and finally it was late afternoon. Amber was already at the big house and was getting things ready for evening in the game room. She was having a hard time trying to think of an idea to get him outside so they could get his picture. She was getting nervous as she walked to the window and saw Paul drive up. All of a sudden she got an idea and she hurried out the door. Paul was just getting out of his car as he saw her coming.

"I need to talk to you for a minute," she said as she walked towards the car. She stepped up and stood in a position so Paul would be facing up the street as they talked.

"What do you need?" he asked.

"Well," she said, "I appreciate you signing for me to get a car, but Vickie doesn't know it yet. She doesn't even know I got a car. I've been parking it a block away so she wouldn't' know. I want to know if you will go and talk to her and tell her."

"Are you kidding me? he said. "Not on your life! You just keep parking down the street. That's one problem I don't need right now."

"Then you won't do it?" Amber said, stalling for more time.

"No," Paul repeated. "She's a pain in the butt." He turned and started walking towards the big house. Amber then went in hoping they got his picture.

It was late when Amber got home. She very softly touched Kim and woke her up. "Tomorrow, when you get a chance and you're over at Rachel's, call Jenkins and see if they got the picture." She then went to bed.

The next day, while Kim was over at Rachel's, she called Mr. Jenkins. "Did you get the picture?" she asked.

"Everything came out good," he told her. "Remember: mums the word. We have to keep this quiet, so he doesn't skip."

"Ok," Kim said, and they hung up.

Kim and Rachel went up to the malt shop and guess who was sitting there? Jeff. Kim hadn't seen him for a couple of days and he seemed to be a little more up beat since the loss of his friend Jimmie.

"Hi," he said as they sat down at the booth with him.

"I haven't seen you for a while," Kim said. "I thought maybe you were mad or something."

"No," he said, staring into space for a moment. "No," he said again, "I've just been floating around."

The girls ordered a drink as they were talking. Jeff asked Kim, "Where did you get all your money? You got a job or something?"

"Well, sort of," Kim answered. "I work around the church with Rachel and we get paid for it."

"Well, that's better than I'm doing."

Then he asked Kim, "Do you remember Tony, the guy I used to bum around at school with?"

"Yes."

"Well he wants to go out camping one of these days. He's got a girlfriend now and she likes to hike and camp, so I was wondering if you'd want to go? It'll be a lot of fun."

"You mean go out and camp all night?" Kim asked.

"Sure," Jeff said.

"I don't think I can do that," Kim said looking at Rachel.

"Why?" Jeff said. "There's nothing wrong with that."

"I'll have to think about it," she said.

"Ok," he said as he started getting fidgety. He couldn't sit still, and all of a sudden he stood up and said, "Well, I've gotta go. I'll see you later." Kim knew that he needed a fix. She had learned enough about him from his mother, watching her sister and Vickie, to know the symptoms.

Kim and Rachel finished their sodas and were walking down the street towards Rachel's home, when Kim reached out and grabbed Rachel's arm and stopped her. She stared at her for a minute. "What's the matter?" Rachel asked.

Kim said, "Rachel, you're the best and closest friend I have, even though we haven't known each other very long. I need someone I can share a secret with that I can trust not to tell anyone and maybe give me some advice on what to do."

"Ok," Rachel said. "I feel the same about you as a friend. I'll help if I can. What's the matter?"

Kim looked at her for a moment as they walked, and finally she just stopped walking and looked Rachel right in the eyes and said, "Jeff's mom asked me to help her with Jeff. He's on drugs pretty bad and it's getting out of control. He's stealing things to sell because his allowance isn't enough to meet his addiction. She's afraid his desperation will reach a point where he's going to get into some real trouble he can't get out of and she thinks, because he likes me, I might be able to get him to stop. I don't know where to start or what do."

Rachel said nothing as they walked along and then stopped. She suddenly turned to Kim and said, "Before we moved here, when I was a lot younger, my mom and dad used to help out at a drug rehabilitation house in their spare time, when dad wasn't preaching. Mom worked there and helped out all the time and dad whenever he could. We could talk to her and maybe she could give you some advice."

"That would be great," Kim said. "Let's go see her now if you think it would be ok."

"Sure," said Rachel and they took off for Rachel's house.

CHAPTER 21

Beverly was just sitting and resting when Rachel and Kim came in the door.

"Hi, Mom," Rachel said as they approached her.

"What's up?" Beverly asked, wondering why the girls were home so early.

"Kim would like to have your advice on a personal problem she has, but it has to remain confidential. Will you help her?" Rachel asked.

"Well, I'll try," Beverly said, looking at Kim, "and it will be just between us, ok?"

"Ok," Kim said. Kim sat down, thought for a moment and said, "You know that boy Jeff I've been seeing; well, he has a drug problem that's getting real bad. His mom doesn't know what to do, so she asked me to help him. She can't do anything for him. He won't listen to her and she's scared he'll do something and get into real trouble because of the drugs he's is getting out of control. I just don't know what to do," Kim said looking at Beverly with desperation on her face.

Beverly was quiet for a second and then asked, Isn't he the same boy whose friend killed himself a few weeks ago?"

"Yes," Kim answered. "His mother is scared that he might do something like that because of the depressive moods he goes into. His parents are divorced and she thinks it's all her fault for not listening to her husband when he was trying to tell her what he was doing. She just couldn't believe it. Now she's desperate."

Beverly looked searchingly at Kim for a moment and said, "You really like that boy don't you?"

"Well, yes," Kim said, "but not like I used to. I don't know why, maybe it's because of what I see it's doing to my sister. I just don't know, but I would like to help him if I could."

Beverly smiled as she said, "It's a very complex world we live in today. During the depression of the 20's and 30's, people used alcohol to drown their problems or make them feel happy till it wore off. Some people became alcoholics and that was all they lived on, and usually ended up destroying their liver and kidneys. Today they use drugs of different kinds to draw out their hurt and pain from the pressure we live in. The problem with drugs is that it destroys the brain in different ways depending on what they are using, and the brain is the most important and powerful part of our body. When it gets damaged, then we are in real trouble. You can't think straight because you're mind is compromised in an altered world that doesn't exist. The drugs keep doing damage to your mind every time you use them until it reaches the level where your problems are no longer a concern. Like alcohol to an alcoholic, addiction to drugs becomes your first priority; you have to have them. You cannot do without them, because you think you're going to go out of your mind. You now need them just to keep your sanity. Your brain is the most powerful weapon in your body. It controls your every thought and emotion and when it's out of whack you're in serious trouble, unless you get help to stop it. If you don't, then ultimately the drugs will kill you. Since you don't know how long Jeff's been on drugs, it's kind of difficult to know how to start." Then Beverly asked Kim, "Has he ever said he's tired of drugs or does he totally deny he's ever used them?"

"He totally denies it," Kim said. "He gets offensive if you ask him anything about it."

"That's not good," Beverly said. "That tells me he's been at it a long time. His mother thinks only bad kids use drugs, so she thinks that he must have been bad. That's not true; a child from a very good home could go to school, make friends and they might be on drugs or running with a group that are on drugs and very innocently get caught up in it."

Then Beverly said, "You don't want to attack him about it. Be his friend; only talk about it when he opens the door. Don't preach, just let him know you care about him and then as time passes and he learns to trust you, maybe then he will open up and you can find a way to reach him. It may take a long time. You'll have to be patient."

"Thank you," Kim said. "You've been a big help. I didn't know where to start."

Rachel and Kim left the house and headed to the church hall where they had some work to do getting ready for a wedding reception. As they worked, they talked. Kim finally said, "I think I'll go camping with Jeff and his friends. Maybe that would help open the door to his feelings and other things that might help me to help him."

"Are you sure you want to do that?" Rachel asked. "With drugs involved, I'd be scared."

"I'm not scared," Kim said. "I'll be all right."

After they finished their work, Rachel headed back home and Kim went looking for Jeff. She headed for the shopping center where she knew he hung out with a bunch of guys. She finally arrived and sure enough, there he was, standing by his car, laughing and joking with his friends.

As Kim approached them, all eyes were on her because she was really pretty. Jeff had a surprised look on his face as he asked her, "What are you doing here?"

"Looking for you," Kim said. "Can I talk to you?"

"Sure," Jeff said.

"Alone," Kim said and looked him straight in the eyes. The guys whooped and hollered and Jeff gave them the finger behind his back as they walked away.

Kim stopped and said, "I've decided to go camping with you and your friend, but I haven't made up my mind whether I'll spend the night or not."

"Ok," Jeff said smiling. "I'll see you later; I gotta go," he said, waving to her as he walked away. It made Kim angry that he just walked away and left her standing. She knew why he did it because his friends were watching and he was showing off.

Meanwhile back at Jenkins office, he was sitting at his desk looking at two pictures he had of Paul Messer, Vickie's so called boyfriend, when

Jordan Willis walked in. Dave stood up, shook his hand and handed him the pictures. Willis looked at them and grinned from ear to ear. He opened his brief case and took out some pictures and papers.

"Look at this," he said as he showed them to Jenkins. Jenkins looked at the pictures and Willis pointed out things on them. "Look here," he said to Jenkins, "This picture was taken in Chicago. See the two men with him. They were the ones the law was after. No one knew who he was. In this picture," as he pointed out another one, "the law was after the man and a woman, but they didn't know who the guy was. He wasn't wanted for anything. Then look at another one here. This is your Vickie and the guy. At that time she was the only one the law wanted. That's been a few years back, before she ever came to this town, and this is your Paul, if that is even his real name, standing with her. One thing I'm sure of," Willis said, "these two are slick operators. They're always on the outside looking in while somebody else is taking the fall." Then Willis stood silent, in deep thought for a moment, and said, "I think we should call in the vice squad on this. Dan Barshaw is the head Bulldog down there. I'll call and arrange a meeting with him if you agree."

"Agreed," said Jenkins. "Do it as soon as possible."

Willis made the call and the meeting was set up for the following morning at Jenkins' office.

Barshaw and Willis arrived at Jenkins' office. After Willis introduced him, they got right down to business. Barshaw went over the information they had. He looked hard at the picture of Paul Messer. "I've seen that guy somewhere before. I'll have to check him out when I get back to my office." Then he looked hard at the picture of Vickie and said, "I've seen her before, too."

Barshaw stared into space as if his mind was some place else. "If we have what I think we have, we might be on to something bigger than we realize. I'll call you tomorrow," he said, and then left.

Jenkins looked at Willis and said, "I know it's a terrible thing to say but I'm glad she's dirty – I mean Vickie. It helps me with what I'm doing."

The next day Jenkins got a call from Willis. "Dave," he said, "I got a call from Barshaw. He checked them out nationwide to see how much information he could find about them. He's heard and seen enough that he doesn't want to touch them yet. He wants to keep them under tight surveillance for as long as it takes to see just how big an operation they have or what higher level operation could be taken out along with them. So far right now, it's their baby. You and me will have to back off for now."

"All right," Jenkins said. "Thanks for calling."

Jenkins then called the court house and asked for Judge Ryan. "This is Dave," he said. He filled the Judge in on what was happening with Vickie and the Judge said, "Well, in light of these things, I think we will just put a stay on ruling on Colden's will till this is over, so don't worry, I'll work it out," and hung up.

It was later in the day when Amber parked her car down the street and walked home. It was a little early yet to go to work, but she didn't have anything else to do. As she walked in the house, she found Vickie was gone. There was a note on the table. It read, 'I've gone shopping for a while', and in big letters, on the bottom, it said '*DON'T TOUCH NOTHIN, Signed Vickie.*'

Amber smiled. It was a relief not to have to deal with her for a little while. As she went in her room, her need for drugs was coming on strong. She looked in her purse and she didn't realize she was out. She went into Vickie's room and opened the drawer looking for her stash. She opened a box and found what she wanted. As she put the box back her hand bumped something else buried under some clothes. She dug it out and opened it up. It was an envelope loaded with money. More money than Amber had ever seen at one time. She thumbed through it and figured there was roughly five thousand dollars. Her eyes about jumped out of her head. Where did Vickie get all this money?

She wondered. She closed it up, put it back and went to her room to start getting ready for work.

CHAPTER 22

The next morning Mr. Jenkins was back in his office preparing his work load for the day, when the phone rang. His secretary answered and said, "It's Judge Ryan."

Jenkins picked up the phone and said, "Hello Judge, to what do I owe the honor?"

"I have decided to release Jake Moran from the honor camp, and parole him in your custody. I know it's sooner than you expected, but I had to make a good show in court. That is what you wanted so now you got him. Good luck," and the judge hung up. That caught Jenkins by surprise as he wondered what would happen next.

The next day Dave Jenkins got in his car and headed to the honor camp where Jake was held.

When he got there, he was taken to a room where he met with Jake and gave him some papers to sign about the rules and regulations Jake had to abide by while on probation. After they went over all the rules, Jenkins said, "You make sure you call me everyday. You miss one time and you'll pay the consequences. One other thing," Jenkins said, "if you cause Amber any more hurt and pain than she already has, I'll throw you to the wolves, do you understand?"

"Yeah," Jake said, "I understand."

Jake got up and started to walk away when Mr. Jenkins said, "Wait a minute." Jake stopped, turned and looked at him. Jenkins said, "If it's as dangerous for you as you say, then you better lay low for a while. Do you have a friend you can trust that you and I can make contact through, especially when you have to report in? You've got enough problems the way it is."

"Jimbo," Jake said. "You can find him through Amber."

Jenkins continued, "We've got to find a place for you to hide, that no one knows about. The only one you make contact with is Jimbo, and me, if it's important. Stay away from Amber, and don't communicate with her — for her own protection, ok?"

"Yeh," Jake said and went on his way. Jenkins headed back to town.

The next morning, as Jenkins entered his office, his phone rang. He answered it before his secretary could get it. It was Jake.

"Mr. Jenkins," he said, "I have an aunt, my mom's sister. Her name is Mabel; her husband's name is Ben Lovejoy. They have a farm about 30 miles out of town. It's really hidden from any main highways." Jake hesitated a moment and said, "but there's a problem. They don't exactly like me, but maybe if you call them, maybe you can talk them into letting me stay with them. They have a little shack down by the barn I could stay in."

Jenkins thought for a moment and then said, "All right — give me their number."

Jenkins hung up the phone and just sat and pondered the situation. No telling what they might think or feel. He felt sure they probably knew about all the trouble Jake had been in, especially since his mother died. He picked up the phone and called.

Mabel answered, "Hello."

"Is this Mrs. Mabel Lovejoy?" he asked.

"Yes, it is," she said.

"My name is Dave Jenkins; I'm an attorney and I represent your nephew Jake Moran. I'm also his parole officer and I need your help concerning Jake."

"What's he done now?" she said in a stern voice.

"He just got out of honor camp," Jenkins said, "and he needs a quiet place to stay for a while until we can work out some of his other problems."

"Oh, no!" Mabel yelled in the phone. "He's not staying here. That kid's so deep in drugs, and I've got two young children, and I don't want him around them. Do you hear me? No, no, no!"

Jenkins said, "But Mrs. Lovejoy, you're all Jake has. What if there's a chance we can help straighten him out? I really need your help."

Mabel was quiet for a moment and said, "I don't want Jake living here, but I'll let you talk to my husband. He'll have to make the decision. He's right here" and she handed the phone to him.

He answered, "This is Ben."

Jenkins explained the situation to him as he did to Mabel. Ben said, "Let me talk to my wife about it and I'll call you back."

"All right," Jenkins said. He gave Ben his number and thanked him for his time.

Ben hung up the phone, looked at his wife and said, "You really don't want him here, do you?"

"No, I don't, "Mabel said. "Look, I loved my sister. She was so sweet and trusting, we were very close. You know that. But she married a son of a bitch who lived off her, beat her, and treated her like scum. She bore him a child and look at what he's turned out to be."

Ben put his hand on her shoulder and said, "Honey, I really don't want him around the kids, either, because of the drugs. But no matter how we feel, remember Jake as young boy growing up, with just him and his mother after his father disappeared. They were very close; all the things Jake did — no matter how bad they were — was so he could help take care of her. He loved her very much. He would have robbed a bank if he had to, to help her."

Mabel blinked the tears back and said, "I loved her too. We'll do it, if that's what you want, Ben, but he scares me. Jake's changed since his mother died," Mabel said. "He's not the same. I don't know if anything can save him now."

Ben called Mr. Jenkins back and told him they would take a chance with Jake, but one false move, he was out. Jenkins thanked Ben and told him he would make all the arrangements.

Two days later, Jenkins picked up Jake and took him to the Lovejoy farm. Jake's car was also taken away from him, as well as the money back when he was arrested. He had no wheels. Mabel came out to meet them.

As Jake got out of the car, he made eye contact with Mabel. "Hi," he said in a gentle voice, for he always liked her, even if she didn't like him. He admired his Uncle Ben because he was a good man who took care of and loved his family, something his own father never was.

Jenkins walked around the car and joined them. Mabel finally said, "Come on, I'll show you where you can stay." They walked towards the hay barn where inside was a very old tiny bunkhouse, but it was very well kept. As they walked in, Jake remembered the house from when he was a little boy. Sometimes he and his mom would stay there when his father was out of control. When things cooled down, they would go home. It had been a long time since he had been back.

"This will be fine. Thank you," he said. He looked at her and smiled. At that moment Mabel remembered no matter how much trouble Jake got into, he was always polite. She took him into the kitchen that was very small and showed him the food she put in the cabinets and refrigerator.

As Mabel and Mr. Jenkins started to go out the door, she turned around and said, "Jake, I don't want you around my children. I don't hate you, but I know your problems and I will do whatever I have to, to protect them, do you understand?"

"Yes," Jake said as he just looked down at the floor.

As Mabel and Jenkins reached his car, Mabel said, "That's the first time I've seen him in a long time. He's turned out to be quite handsome. He looks so much like his mom. She was quite pretty. He also has her tenderness and gentleness. God, why does life have to be so complicated? I'd like to love him, but I'm afraid to."

"I understand," Jenkins said. "The reason I'm helping him is because his girl friend begged me to. Her parents are both dead and I'm looking after her and her sister. They're very good girls who had a wonderful mother and father. Her name is Amber. Right now Jake is her whole life, no matter what he's done. He treats her like a queen."

Mabel smiled and said good-bye and Jenkins drove away. Mabel went in the house and grabbed her purse. She was heading for her car when she stopped, thought a second, and then went back in the house, went to a cabinet in the laundry room and took out a box. Then she headed for the bunkhouse. She knocked on the door and Jake answered. "Here," she said as she walked in. She opened the box and took out a telephone, walked over and plugged it into a phone outlet on the wall. "The phone line is connected to our phones in the house. You are not to use it for anything except emergencies. I'm going into town for a while to shop until school is out. Then I'll pick up the kids and come home. Ben might be home by then. I don't know for sure," and she left.

CHAPTER 23

J ake checked the bunkhouse out. He found some old magazines and books lying around. Then he went outside to look around. He walked around the barn, looking at horses and a couple of steers. Then he saw an old pick-up truck parked by the tractor. He went over to get a better look at it. It was old, but looked like it was in pretty good shape. He noticed it didn't have any license plates, which meant it was just a farm truck, not driven on public roads. He opened the door and noticed the key was in the dash. He got in, turned the key and it started right up. It sounded pretty good, Jake thought. He turned it off, got out and continued wandering around the farm.

At the Colden home, Vickie was sitting in the kitchen when Kim walked in the door. She sat down across from Vickie and they just stared at each other. Then Kim said, "I've been invited to go on a campout Saturday evening. Would that be all right?"

Vickie looked at her for a moment, thinking about the mess they had a couple of weeks ago over the dog. "Ok," Vickie said, "under one condition. I don't want to hear anymore about that damn dog of yours. Do you understand?"

"All right," Kim said. She got up and walked away for she thought, I'll never forgive her for killing my dog. She went in her room and searched her closet for her sleeping bag, just in case she needed it.

Vickie yelled at her through the door. "I'm going out for a while. Lock the door if you leave. I don't know when I'll be back."

"Ok," Kim yelled back.

Jeff had picked his friend Tony up and was cruising around just for something to do. "Are you ready for Saturday night?" Jeff asked him.

"Yep," Tony replied, as he reached in his pocket and pulled out a mushroom.

"What the hell are you doing with them damn things?" Jeff asked, very disgusted. "Those things make you crazy. How many times I got to tell you?"

"You're not telling me anything," Tony said. "These things beat coke all to hell. Mushrooms are for men who want to have a really good time."

"You think you're a man, huh?" Jeff said.

"Yeah, I'm a man," said Tony. Jeff looked at him disgustedly and just shook his head.

Since Amber started working Kim didn't see much of her, especially since Amber had her own car. Neither of them liked hanging around the house any more than they had to. Their hatred of Vickie went beyond words, and the less they saw of her, the better they felt. Kim spent most of her time with Rachel. They had such a kindred spirit that you would think they were sisters.

Rachel asked, "Kim, are you really going to go camping with Jeff?"

"Yeh, I guess," Kim answered.

"Why?" Rachel asked. "You know he's doing drugs. You know there's always trouble wherever he's at. You know the kind of people he runs with. Why?"

"I know," Kim answered. "I know he lies all the time to cover his tracks. But he wasn't like that until he started doing drugs. I promised his mother that I would try to help him," she reminded Rachel. "Maybe the camping trip will help me to find a way to reach him."

Rachel just shrugged her shoulders. Then she reached out and touched Kim's hand and said, "Who am I to judge. Maybe you can help him. Only God knows how it's all going to work out."

"You really put a lot of faith in God, don't you?" Kim said.

"Yes," Rachel answered. "Dad told me that the way the world is now, we need God on our side more than ever. He says if we allow him, he will guide us through all hell, no matter what."

"How is that done?" Kim asked.

Rachel looked at Kim for a moment. "You ask him. You let God know that you believe and trust in him. You ask him to forgive you for your sins —you know, the bad things you've done or thought in your mind. You ask him to come into your life and guide you and help you through all your trials. Let him know that you believe in him and his son Jesus, and anything else you might want to tell him."

Kim looked at Rachel with tears in her eyes and said, "Will you help me?"

"Yes," Rachel said as the tears welled up in her eyes also. They knelt down by the bed and prayed. When they were done, they stood up and hugged each other, and now they were even closer in their relationship. As they stood wiping their tears away, Kim couldn't help but think about Amber, her sister. She wished she knew how to help her.

Then Rachel said, "Remember Kim, we're just human beings, we're just natural born sinners and even though you want to do the right things, you'll still screw up now and then. When that happens, you ask God to forgive you, and he will.

No matter how many times you screw up, he'll forgive you."

Kim smiled and said, "I'll see you later. I got some other things to do to get ready for the camping trip."

As Kim turned to leave, Rachel reached out and touched her and said, "There's something else you have to do which can be very hard."

"What's that?" Kim asked.

"You have to forgive those who have hurt you," Rachel told her.

"That's impossible," Kim answered. "I can't do that."

"You have to try, Kim, and keep trying. That's one of the laws of God's Love. He forgives you so you have to forgive also." Kim didn't answer her. She just stared at Rachel and then left.

Kim reached home and went in. As she headed toward her room she saw Vickie sitting at the kitchen table, with her head resting on the table, an empty whiskey glass by her hand. Kim stopped and stared at her for a minute, wondering how she could ever forgive her after what she'd done, then went into her room.

Back at the Lovejoy's farm, Jake was totally bored. With his aunt and uncle working, and the kids in school, he had nothing to do but sit around and read or just walk around the farm. Ben, his uncle finally arrived home from work. Jake walked up to him and asked him if there was anything he could do. "I'm going nuts with nothing to do."

Ben looked at him for a moment and said, "You're pretty mechanical, If I remember right."

"Right," Jake said.

"Let's go out to the other barn. I got something to show you." As they entered the barn Jake saw a very old tractor. It looked pretty good. Ben looked at Jake and said, "It's an old bugger, a lot older then you and me. I've kept it around for a lot of years, since my dad died, hoping that someday I could work on it and get it running again. Sort of an antique. If we got it running and gave it a coat of paint it would look pretty good. Do you want to tackle it?" he asked.

"Hell yes," Jake said. "Boy, that'll be a lot of fun

"Good," Ben said. "All my tools are in the shed. You know where they are, so when ever you want, just have at it."

"Thanks," Jake said and went over to the tool shed to see what kind of tools his uncle had. He went in and looked around at everything. He was amazed at all the tools Ben had. He didn't realize it took so many to run a farm. Most auto shops didn't have as many tools as Ben had.

The next morning Jake got all the tools he needed and started working on the tractor. He decided to go through the engine first to see if he could get it running and then fix all the things that would be needed. As the day passed by Jake had another problem he had to solve. He was addicted to cocaine. While he was in the honor camp he made connections with the other prisoners to get drugs, but he didn't have access out at the farm. It was starting to get the best of him. He couldn't concentrate on what he was doing. He needed some coke really bad. He had promised Ben and Mabel that he would try to clean up and behave himself while he was living with them, but he was getting so desperate now he no longer could think about that. He had to find a way to get some coke before he went out of his mind. As the days passed his withdrawals grew worse.

In town, Kim finally finished getting her stuff together It was a couple more days before they were going camping, so she hung around over Rachel's house most of the time, but this morning as she arrived at the Hardings', Rachel had some news for Kim.

"We're not leaving as soon as we thought," Rachel said. "The church can't find a replacement for my dad, so we will probably stay for another month. That means I'll have to start school here till we can move."

"Good," Kim said. "I'm really going to miss you guys. I don't know what I'm going to do when you leave. You're my best friend."

Back at the farm, Jake couldn't handle it anymore. He called Jimbo, who was supposed to call only when he had to make contact with Mr.

Jenkins. "Jimbo, I need some coke, can you get me some?"

"Gee," Jimbo said, "I'm out, too. I got fired from my job last week and I'm broke. They caught me sniffing coke."

"I gotta have some," Jake said desperately.

"Wait," Jimbo said, "I probably could get some from Amber. She's got a good job now, she makes good money. She's even got a car."

"Really," Jake answered. Jake wanted to see Amber badly. He knew the consequences if Jenkins found out, but he didn't care. "Ok," Jake said to Jimbo. "Find out if she could meet some day around noon at the old building by the school."

"How you gonna get here?" Jimbo asked.

"I'll find a way," Jake said. "Just ask her and I'll call back tomorrow." Jake figured that noon was the best time he could leave, when everybody was gone in the morning, and get back before they got home. His only problem now was figuring out how to get to town and back. Meanwhile he went back to work on the tractor.

CHAPTER 24

Jimbo drove past Amber's house. He was in luck he found her walking down the sidewalk to her car parked a block away. He pulled up to the curb, rolled the window down and yelled, "Hi, Amber. You got a minute?"

"Sure," she said as she stepped over to his car.

"I spoke with Jake," Jimbo said.

Amber's eyes got real big. "Where, when?"

"Well he's not allowed to see or talk to you, but he wants to see you anyway."

Then Amber came to her senses and asked, "Is he out of honor camp? How come he's not allowed to see me?"

"Yes, he's out," Jimbo said, "but I don't know why he's not allowed to see you. He wants to meet you at the old building across from the school on whatever day you can, about noon."

"Tomorrow," she said excitedly.

"Tomorrow, ok," Jimbo said. "I'll let him know." Jimbo hesitated, then said, "He needs some coke."

The next morning after everyone was gone, Jake called Jimbo. "Yeah, she'll meet you today if you can get there," he said.

"Tell her I'll try," Jake said and hung up. Jake walked around the house wondering how he was going to get to town. He knew the only vehicle around was the old pick-up truck, but it didn't have any license plates on it. Then he thought, if he took all back country farm roads and stayed off the main highway he shouldn't run into any cops. Then when he got to town, he would stay away from the main part of town and come in on the road off the back side of the old building in the alley. About 10:30 Jake quit working on the tractor, cleaned his hands, jumped in the old truck and took off.

Amber was in a coffee shop with one of the girls who worked at the big house. As they drank coffee and talked, Amber kept watching the time. As it approached 11:00 am, she said, "I have to get going; I'll see you later," and got up and left.

Jake got there first and parked the truck in a place in the alley he thought nobody would see it. He went to the place he used to always meet her. Finally Amber showed up, driving down the main street, parking in front of the building and heading in. She was very excited; she hadn't seen him for such a long time. She entered the spot where Jake was. As soon as she saw him, she ran up to him and jumped in his arms. They kissed and hugged for a couple of minutes. When they came up for air, Jake asked "You got any coke? I need some real bad. I'm about to go crazy."

"Sure," Amber said as she took a little packet out of her pocket and gave it to him. Jake was so nervous he almost dropped the bag. "I got more," Amber said as Jake stood there taking deep snorts of coke. Amber asked, "So where are you staying? Why are you hiding? Why can't I see you?"

"Because that's the way Jenkins says it has to be. If the guys I owe the money to knew I was out, they would be looking for me, and I can't pay them. They might kill me. But I couldn't stand not seeing you and I needed some coke really bad."

"How much do you need?" Amber asked.

"Four Thousand dollars," Jake said.

"Wow!" She said. "It would take forever to raise that kind of money at my job."

"What kind of job you got?" Jake asked.

"I serve drinks and food at a high class dining room," Amber lied. She didn't want him to know the truth.

"If I don't find a way to come up with that money, I'm going to be in really big trouble," he said, staring off into space.

Amber went up and kissed him and said, "We will figure something out."

"I sure hope so," Jake said and kissed her back.

They spent almost an hour together making out and talking when Jake said, "I have to go. I have to get back to my Aunt's house. It's a little farm a ways out of town down the highway. I have to get the truck back before they get home or I'm in big trouble. Let's meet again in a couple of days," Jake said, "about the same time. Would that be ok?"

"Yes," Amber said, "I'll be here." They kissed and went their separate ways. As Amber drove away she was really worried about Jake. She knew it was a lot worse than what Jake was telling her and she just didn't know how to help him.

Jake arrived back at farm, and quickly got to work on the old tractor. With his addiction satisfied for now, he could think more clearly about what he was doing.

Friday came and Kim was all packed and ready to go. Jeff would be picking her up around 4:00 pm. The time was getting close as she waited for him. She sat on her bed and then got up and walked back and forth, then sat down again. She was a little nervous because she had never been camping before with anyone, and didn't know what to expect. Finally he pulled up and honked his horn twice. She grabbed her stuff and headed out the door. She never stopped to look for Vickie, she just left. Jeff got out and helped her get her stuff in the car. Kim noticed how calm he was, so she figured he had a fix.

"I noticed a tent bag in the trunk," Kim said. "I told you I hadn't made up my mind."

"I know," Jeff said. "I brought it along just in case. Ok?" Kim didn't answer.

They finally arrived at the camp ground. Kim noticed the camp ground was not too far from the main highway. Jeff noticed Kim looking back at the highway.

"They built that highway right through the middle of the camping area a few years ago," he said. "Stupid, stupid," he repeated.

As they finished getting everything unloaded, another car drove up. It was Tony with his girl-friend, Mona. Tony was about 6 ft. tall and average looking. He dressed in very loud, colorful clothes and had a hunting knife in a sheath hanging on his belt. Mona was about as tall as Kim, not nearly as pretty, but she sure had a body that wouldn't quit and she dressed to show it off. It embarrassed Kim a little when she was introduced to her. They unloaded their cars.

Tony started setting up his tent when Jeff hollered at him, "Hey, did you bring some more wood?"

"Yeah," Tony answered, "I got a bunch in the trunk."

Jeff stacked his wood near the fire pit. Then he started setting up his tent. That made Kim very uneasy. Jeff just looked at her with a smile but didn't say anything. Tony took all the wood out of his car and stacked it on top of the rest. Jeff got a fire going and then sat back and watched it burn. Kim and Mona spread a large cloth on the ground and put the food and utensils on it. Jeff set the cooler down near the food. They all got a cold drink out of the cooler and sat around laughing and talking as they watched the fire burning down to get hot enough coals to roast their hot dogs over. All of a sudden Jeff got up and crawled into his tent. After a few minutes he came back and got involved again. Kim knew why he left: he needed a fix.

Finally the coals burned down and they started cooking their food. Kim was relaxing more as she was starting to enjoy herself. Jeff spread out another blanket on the ground a short distance from the fire. Tony did the same thing for himself and Mona about 30 ft away. It was starting to get pretty dark so they both lit their kerosene lanterns and set them near their blankets.

Tony went over to the cooler and took out two cans of beer for him and Mona. Jeff said, "Yeah," and got up and got two beers also. He started to hand one to Kim, but she refused it.

"Go ahead," Jeff said, "you'll like it."

"No I won't," Kim said.

"When did you ever taste beer?" Jeff asked.

"When I was younger — my dad let me taste it and it was horrible."

"Yeah," Jeff said, "it doesn't taste so good when you first drink it, but if you keep drinking it, you'll grow to like it."

"I don't want to grow to like it," Kim said. "Give me a Pepsi." Jeff just shook his head in disgust, turned and put the beer back in the cooler and got her a Pepsi. As they sat on the blanket, Jeff leaned over and kissed Kim. Then he kissed her again. This time she kissed him back.

While they were making out, Kim pulled away from him. He looked at her kind of puzzled, and Kim said, "How much do you really care about me?"

What Jeff heard kind of startled him. She said again, "How much do you care for me... or am I just another one of your girls?"

"No," Jeff said, "you're the only one."

Kim was silent for a moment and then leaned close to him and said, "Do you care enough to quit doing drugs?"

Jeff quickly sat up straight, looked at her hard and said, "Ok man, all I ever do is smoke a little grass now and then."

"Jeff I know what you're on, I've known for a long time. I want you to quit using drugs."

"You don't know what you're talking about," he said angrily. "My mom put that stuff in your head, didn't she, right?"

"She told me some things," Kim said, trying to be calm. "But it wasn't anything I didn't already know."

"Ok, you think you know everything, huh?" he said.

"You didn't answer my question," Kim said. "Would you try to quit for me?" Jeff turned away from her looking down, shaking his head in disgust. He looked up, staring across the fire at Tony and he saw him take a little bag out of his pocket. He opened it, took something out and ate it. Jeff knew what it was — a mushroom, the very thing he had told him not to bring.

"Oh, God," he murmured.

"What's the matter?" Kim asked.

"Nothing," he said. "Nothing, nothing." Then Tony and Mona got up and crawled into the tent. You could hear them taking their clothes off. Kim knew what was happening and she was getting very uneasy. Jeff noticed, so he tried to take her attention away from that.

"Ok," he said, "if you want me to quit, then I'll quit if it'll make you happy, ok?"

"Ok," Kim said, not really believing him.

"Fine, that's all settled then," he said as he reached over and kissed her. Then he put his hand on her breast.

"I'm not ready to do that," Kim said, pushing his hand away.

"It'll be ok," Jeff said softly. "The first time is always a little scary, but after that it's easy. I promise you'll like it," Jeff said as he put his hand on her breast again.

"I said no," and she pushed his hand away again.

"Come on, Kim," Jeff said. "We didn't come out here just to stare at the stars. You knew that."

"I didn't know anything of the kind," Kim said. "I told you before I wasn't ready for that and I meant it."

Jeff sat back, frustrated, when they heard a scream from Mona. "What's the matter with you?"

she screamed again as she quickly crawled out of the tent. She was half naked and was bleeding.

"Are you crazy?" she screamed again. Tony crawled out behind her. All he had on was his underwear. He grabbed her by the leg, laughing like a crazy man with a herky jerky sound. He had his knife out and he stabbed her again. She pulled away and the knife went in her arm. The blood poured out of her, she was screaming in agony.

Jeff quickly ran over to them while Kim sat in shock, watching. Jeff grabbed Tony and pulled him away from Mona, yelling, "What's the matter with you? I told you not too eat those damn things, didn't I? Look what you've done!" he hollered. Tony was still laughing as he rammed the knife into Jeff's stomach. Then he pulled it out and stabbed him again and again. Jeff fell to the ground with his eyes wide open and in total shock. He didn't move. Tony was still laughing loudly as he looked at Kim.

Kim was far enough away that she was able to get up and start running as fast as she could towards the highway. She was screaming and crying as she ran. She looked back and could barely see in the dark if Tony was chasing her. She could still hear him laughing hysterically in the distance. She finally reached the highway totally exhausted. She was screaming, crying and waving her hands in the head lights of the cars and trucks going by, but no one stopped. Finally a patrol car came by and saw her. They turned their red lights on and pulled over. They tried to calm her down and finally she was able to talk and tell them what happened. They grabbed their flash lights, pulled their guns and started down the hill carefully searching the darkness for Tony. They finally reached the fire pit still burning and there was Tony, laughing and going around in circles with his arms in the air and the knife in his hand.

"Drop the knife," one of the policemen said. Tony continued to dance around the fire in his underwear as if no one was around but him. The police could see both Mona and Jeff lying on the ground not moving. They repeated to him to drop the knife, to no avail. As one officer continued to talk to him and held a gun on him, the other officer sneaked around behind him, grabbed his arm, and wrestled the knife away from him. Then he handcuffed him, while the other officer called for an ambulance and back up.

One officer checked Jeff and found he was still breathing. He did everything he could to stop the bleeding. The ambulance arrived and a paramedic loaded Jeff in and tended his wounds. He had lost a whole lot of blood and his wounds were extremely bad. The other officer checked Mona, and she was also still alive. They tried to stop the bleeding and covered her up the best they could until another ambulance arrived. When the officers had everything under control, one of them went and got the patrol car and picked up Kim. He brought her back to the camp site. She started crying uncontrollably. She couldn't stop. It was quite a while before the police could question her.

When the second ambulance arrived, the paramedics tended Mona, put her in, and took her to the hospital. When the officer searched Tony's clothes in the tent, they found the little bag with the mushrooms in it. That pretty much revealed what had happened.

Kim asked if she could go to the hospital where they took Jeff, as she cried hysterically. The officer agreed to take her. He put her in the patrol car, turned his siren on and took off. Kim continued to cry uncontrollably as the officer gently tried to question her about the incident. They finally reached the hospital. The officer took her in and walked her to the admission desk. A nurse escorted her and the officer to Jeff's room as she gave updates on his current condition.

Jeff's mother was contacted by the police and when they told her what happened, she screamed over the phone, "No! No!" She dropped the phone, ran out of the house, jumped into her car and took off for the hospital.

When she reached the hospital, she ran in as fast as she could. The nurse quickly identified her as his mother and directed her to his room. He was in the intensive care unit recovering from surgery. As she began to walk into his room, the doctor stopped her and took her around the corner in the hallway. At that point, he informed her that Jeff's wounds were so severe, he did not expect Jeff to live long. When the doctor was finished discussing all the details about Jeff, he allowed her to go into his room.

As she approached his bedside, she took his hand. She didn't see Kim sitting in a chair near the door. She bent over and softly spoke to him; "Jeff honey", she sobbed; "mommy's here". He could barely open his eyes. He tried to speak, but he was so weak, it was just a whisper. His mother put her ear down close to his mouth so she could hear him. "I'm sorry, mom. I'm sorr... and the breath went out of him. He was dead. She screamed and threw herself on him, hugging him and crying: "Jeff! Jeff!" The nurse and doctor pulled her off him and helped her stand up. As she got on her feet shaking and crying, she saw Kim standing and looking at her lost in a crying gaze of unbelievable sadness. She walked over and grabbed Kim, hugging her tight as they both stood grieving and crying.

Later on, the officer took Kim home. He helped her to her door and rang the bell two or three times before Vickie answered it. When Vickie saw the officer, she was filled with fear for a moment and then got it under control. The officer explained to her what happened as she helped Kim to her room. Kim just threw herself across the bed and started crying again.

It was very late when Amber got home. She went in her room, turned on a little night light by her bed and started getting ready for bed, when she thought she heard Kim whimpering. She shook her a little bit and Kim woke up and started to scream. Amber put her hand on her mouth so Vickie wouldn't hear her. "It's me, it's me," Amber said softly. Kim grabbed her and hugged her tightly, crying very softly.

"Oh, Amber," she cried. "Jeff is dead, it was awful."

Amber asked, "What happened?"

"We went camping," Kim said, "with his friend, Tony, and his girl friend, Mona. Tony ate some kind of mushrooms and went crazy. He killed Jeff and he stabbed his girlfriend, too."

When Amber heard the word mushrooms, she said, "Oh my God."

"What am I going to do?" Kim said. "I told Jeff's mom I would try to help Jeff to get off drugs and now he's dead."

"It's not your fault," Amber said. "There is no way you could have known what was going to happen."

Then Kim grabbed Amber and said, "Amber, please quit doing drugs. I don't want to lose you, too. Please, please," she pleaded. Amber didn't answer she just helped Kim get in bed and then went to bed herself.

CHAPTER 25

Morning came and Amber was sound asleep when Kim got up. She went in the bathroom and splashed cold water on her face. Kim's eyes were all swollen from crying so much and she was still shaking all over. She got dressed and headed for Rachel's house. Beverly answered the door. When she opened it, Kim grabbed her and hugged her, and started crying again. Kim told her everything that happened as they sat. Beverly held her close, and then she put her hand on her head and prayed for God to give her the peace that passes all understanding.

Rachel had been standing in one of the doorways listening to everything. The tears were coming from her eyes also. She felt so hurt and sorry for Kim.

Pastor Harding also overheard what was being said. He finally came in the room, put his hand on Kim's head and said, "Would you like me to go see Jeff's mother and see what I can do to help her?"

"Yes, oh yes," Kim said. "Thank you."

The days passed quickly and Jeff's funeral came. After the church service, the pallbearers, friends of Jeff in school, set the casket on the grave site and stepped back into the crowd. Kim noticed most of the crowd were high school students. She realized that Jeff, because of his personality and good looks, was very popular.

Pastor Harding stepped up and looked around at the crowd. He realized there were a lot of young people there with their parents. Then he spoke softly. "We all are feeling very sad and hurt about what happened to this boy. It's incredibly sad. But remember: Jeff is the one in the coffin, yes, but it could be anyone's young son, grandson, nephew or friend. Why? Because, of the uncontrolled drug use among our community's children. The shame of it all is that we have parents on drugs, so how do these poor children have a chance?" He shook his head and then continued. "Lord, the pain of this loss will last a long time. Please help us find a way to stop the drugs destroying our young people and so many other lives. In Jesus name we pray. Amen."

Pastor Harding and Beverly walked over to Kim and Rachel. He put his hand on Rachel's shoulder and said, "We won't be moving for a while longer. The board has finally found a replacement for me, but he can't come for at least two months. So you'll definitely have to start school here. Besides, I know you and Kim will enjoy spending a little more time together." That made Kim and Rachel smile a bit.

Many of the young people came forward and dropped flowers on the coffin. Kim saw Jeff's mother standing and just staring at the grave with tears trickling down her cheek. A man stood with her. Kim walked slowly up to them. "I'm sorry,"

Kim said. "I'm so sorry. I feel like I've failed you and Jeff." Then she began to cry.

Before she could say another word, Jeff's mother put her hands on Kim's cheeks and said, "It's not your fault and you didn't fail at anything. There's no way you could have known this was going to happen. Maybe it just wasn't meant to be. We'll never know. But don't *you* ever feel guilty, do you understand?" She smiled through her tears at Kim.

Then she said, "This is Jeff's father, Darren." He nodded to Kim.

Kim hugged her and told her, "Thank you. I'll never forget you," and then turned and slowly walked away.

Amber was standing a ways back in the crowd. She watched Kim walk over to Rachel, so she decided to leave and talk to her another time. As Amber reached her car, she suddenly broke down crying, so out of control that she could hardly stand. She struggled to get in her car, and just sat and cried.

The next day Jake called Jimbo, and told him to ask Amber if she could meet him at the same place again. He wanted to see her, and he was getting low on cocaine.

Jake came out of the barn where he had been working on the tractor. He didn't realize how late it was. His Uncle Ben was looking at the old truck. He walked around it, looked underneath the back of it, and then he noticed Jake watching him. "Hi," he said to Jake, "Where have you been driving the truck with that mud on it?"

"Oh...probably when I drove it down through the creek bed the other day, just looking around. Sort of taking a break," he said, trying not to look nervous.

"Oh," said Ben. "How you coming with the tractor?"

"Pretty good," Jake said with a big sigh of relief.

Ben went back to the house and Jake went back in the barn, took a deep breath and went to work. He had reached the point when he was going to try to start the engine. He hooked the battery cables up, got on the tractor, and turned the key. Nothing happened, so he got off and checked his wiring and the cables. He got back on and tried to start it again. The motor turned over but wouldn't start. He pulled the choke out farther, pumped the foot feed and turned the key again, put his foot on starter and pushed down hard. The engine started. Jake gleamed with joy. He got off and checked everything out while it was idling.

Ben was in the house fixing a cup of coffee when he heard his wife come home from work with the kids. He took his coffee, walked out the door to greet them. As he walked toward them, he suddenly stopped and was listening real hard staring toward the barn. "What's the matter?" Mabel asked.

Ben responded in a raised voice, with excitement. "Do you hear that? Does he have that old tractor running already? I can hardly believe it. Just listen to that." He walked quickly past his wife without looking at her, heading for the barn.

He rushed in, seeing Jake tinkering with the carburetor as the engine purred. "Fantastic," Ben shouted as he put his hand on Jake's shoulder. "Just fantastic." He repeated.

Jake was stunned, feeling Ben's hand on his shoulder, looking at him with a big smile. It had been a long, long time since he had experienced that kind of feeling towards him other than Amber. He didn't know how to act. He felt kind of funny.

Ben slapped him on the back and said, "You're doing a good job. It's been years since that old tractor ran."

Jake smiled and said, "Now all I got to do is get the clutch, brakes and whatever else needs fixing and we can drive it.

"Ha, ha," Ben laughed as he walked out of the barn and back to the house.

Mabel was in the kitchen as he came in and saw the beaming look on his face. "You've really taken a liking toward Jake, haven't you?"

Ben hesitated for a moment, then he said, "Yeah." He turned to leave the room, then looked back at her and said, "Yeah," again, shaking his head. Mabel went on fixing supper, thinking I'm not ready for that yet.

The next morning Jake went up to the house and had breakfast with Mabel and the kids, before she took them to school and went to work. Jake did something that shocked her. He helped the kids get all of their stuff loaded in the car. He had never done that before. She also saw how her children had come to like him. At that moment she just didn't know how to feel.

"Thanks," Mabel said, getting in the car. As she drove away, she couldn't help thinking about how her husband's attitude towards Jake had changed, and her kids getting friendlier and spending more time around him when they're home. She wondered if this could become a problem, with Jake's background. She knew about his drug problem, but he seemed to be doing pretty good since he came to live with them. Maybe he is trying to change, she thought. Maybe working on the tractor...it's obvious he is enjoying it. Just maybe she thought.

Meanwhile, Jake continued to work on the tractor, thinking he needed to see Amber soon. His craving for coke was getting stronger and he needed a fix soon. It was close to noon and he was getting hungry. He cleaned the grease off his hands and went to lunch. As he was eating, the phone rang. He answered it and it was Jimbo. He informed Jake the day and time Amber would be meeting him at the old building.

Meanwhile, Mr. Jenkins was at his office, busy with some paperwork, when his phone rang. "Hello," he answered. "Hi, this is Willis. I've got some more information for you. We've found there are two more snakes involved with in this thing with your Vickie. They're names are Mitch and Butch. That's all we've got for names at this point, but we think they get their drugs from that Paul fellow. This thing gets bigger all the time." Then Willis said, "If you get a chance, ask Amber if she knows anything about these two guys. Maybe she would be able to help us."

"I doubt that," Jenkins answered. "She's crazy about Jake and I don't think she would tell me anything, even if she knew."

"Well," Willis said, "it's worth a try at the right opportunity. I'll be talking to you," and Willis hung up.

It was the time for Amber to go meet Jake. She parked in front of the old building again and Jake parked in the back like before. They entered the building and found each other in the back near the alley. Amber gave him some coke, they kissed and hugged.

Then Jake said, "I don't think you ought to park out in front. Someone might see you and recognize you."

"All right," Amber said. The time passed as they lingered for a while talking; Jake had to get back before he got caught. He left first and then Amber. As she was going to her car, Mitch and Butch drove by and saw her. Amber didn't notice them. She had only seen them twice: once when she was hiding in the old building, and once talking to Paul. They knew who she was though and they wondered what she was doing there.

School was starting in a couple more days. Mitch and Butch were getting ready in the old building, like Jake did before he got caught. It was a perfect place, so close to the school. They decided to drive around to the back of the building, just looking it over. They turned into the alley at one end of the block, and saw an old truck going fast and turning down the street at the other end. Is it somebody new staking out their territory, or was it just a coincidence? Or was it someone that Amber was associated with? They decided they would keep a close watch on the building to see if anything was going on.

Jake made it back to the farm and immediately went back to work on the tractor. He was getting more enthused about getting the tractor done. He thought, building it thing back like new was just like building back an old car. It would be a classic. His only problem was that he had been on drugs so long it was hard for him to concentrate on what he was doing. There were times he wished he had never heard of or used them. But he knew it was too late now. He was hooked and he couldn't do anything about it.

CHAPTER 26

Meanwhile Amber went home, parked down the street like she always had, and walked to the house. She didn't see Paul parked down around the corner, watching her. He was doing that more often now. He had lost interest in Vickie for sex since besides the drugs, she was becoming more and more of an alcoholic. She was drinking all the time now, besides doing drugs. His lust for Amber was getting stronger and he was having a hard time controlling it. He thought there must be some way to get Vickie out of the house for a while, so he might be able to get to Amber.

When Paul did things, he always made sure there were no witnesses. That is why he wouldn't try anything around the big house. He didn't trust anybody, including Vickie. As he watched Amber disappear into the house, he started hatching a plan in his mind. He would get Vickie to sober up long enough to go in his place on one of his trips, to meet their main drug suppliers. That would get her away from the house for a day or two. That's all the time he needed.

However, there was a problem; Vickie didn't drive anymore. She couldn't stay sober very long and was afraid of being stopped by a cop. That wouldn't be good. But, he thought, she could take a cab to the meeting, which was in another city, not far away. So he sat his plan in motion, all the while his lust for Amber grew even stronger. He finally started his car and drove away.

Meanwhile Amber was getting her clothes together she was going to wear to work at the big house.

The next few days passed quickly and school had finally started. Kim went to meet Rachel and they walked to school together. On that particular day, Amber planned to meet Jake at the old building and bring him some coke. Jake was getting ready to go meet her, as he stood back looking at the tractor he'd been working on. He had it running like a clock, and just about had it all painted. He was starting to feel proud of what he had done. He hadn't felt like that in a long time.

He jumped in the truck and took off. Arriving in the alley behind the old building, he saw Amber was already there. Amber was hiding, and when he walked past her, she jumped out at him and said, "Boo."

He almost jumped out of his skin. He grabbed her and they hugged and kissed. She handed him the coke and they sat on an old wooden box and enjoyed the short amount of time they had together.

Outside, driving around the block and then turning into the alley, were Mitch and Butch, Paul's drug distributors and henchmen of sorts. When they saw the truck, and recognized Amber's car, they stopped and got out of their car. They decided to walk up and sneak a peek through the holes in the walls to see who was with Amber. When they saw Jake, they were shocked, since they thought he was in prison at an honor camp and suppose to be gone for a long time. They quietly went back to their car and left. They decided to go somewhere they could talk and figure out how to get the money Jake owed them. They thought maybe Jake was going to start dealing again, without them. They had no idea what he was doing there. Where would he be getting his drugs? Does he have another source?

"That son-of-a-bitch!" Butch hollered. "Let's just kill him. He ain't ever gonna pay us, let's just kill him."

"No," Mitch said. "Let's try to get our money first. We'll sneak up and trap him, and then see what kind of line he hands us before we do that."

Meanwhile Paul put his plans in motion. He called his drug supplier contact in Burnsville, "Mike, I need a favor. I'm sending my partner Vickie to make the pick up." He asked him to stall her for a couple of days because he had some personal business to attend to. Mike agreed and hung up.

Paul was done making all the arrangements so he called Vickie to be ready. "Pack enough things for at least a couple of days, because it will probably take that long for the transaction. I'll have a cab come and pick you up."

"Why a cab?" Vickie asked. "That's a long way to go in a taxi."

"No one would be suspicious of a cab picking you up instead of a car," Paul said. "Just be ready."

"Smart ass," she said as she hung up. She was not comfortable with the whole idea, and didn't like it. Morning came. The taxicab arrived. The driver loaded Vickie's luggage and she got in.

As the cab drove away, Vickie still couldn't understand why Paul wanted her to go make their drug deal. There were a lot of things puzzling her. Why did Paul want to get into the prostitution business with his big house he started? The drug business was highly profitable. Their profits were channeled into an off shore bank after it had been laundered by another associate of theirs. She didn't know how much money they had because Paul never gave her much information and when he did, he usually talked in circles, never really telling her anything like he used to. She always kept four to five thousand dollars hidden in the house for emergencies that might arise, like getting out of town quick if something went wrong. She was seeing less and less of Paul at night and she wondered if he was having an affair with Amber. Maybe Amber doesn't hate him as much as she lets on. Vickie loved Paul very much, even though she knew he couldn't be trusted where women were concerned. Money was Vickie's god, though, which is why she just couldn't wait to get her hands on the money from John's Will. She loved the fact it would be all hers for the taking. She wouldn't have to share it with anyone. Not even the girls. She couldn't understand why it was taking so long, but she wasn't going to make any waves and cause more delays. She would just play it cool. Vickie pondered all these things as the cab drove down the freeway.

Vickie had been gone about two hours when Paul drove by the house to check things out. Then he drove to a public phone and called Amber. Amber was awake and had just finished getting dressed when she heard the phone ring. She knew Vickie was gone, so she answered it.

"Hello," she said. there was no answer, and then a click as Paul hung up. He drove around the block and parked far enough away that no one would notice him. He was waiting to see where Kim was, to check if she was home or already gone.

In the house, Kim was also dressed and ready to leave. She asked, "Amber, who was that on the phone?"

"I don't know," Amber said. "They just hung up. It must have been a wrong number."

"I'm going over Rachel's," Kim said. "Bye."

"See ya," Amber yelled, as she went out the door.

Paul spotted Kim coming out of the house and heading down the street. That was his cue. He drove around the back and parked in the alley behind the house. Then he snuck quietly to the back door. He had a key Vickie had given him to get in at night when the girls were in bed. As he walked quietly through the house, he heard water running. Amber was in the bathroom fixing her hair and brushing her teeth. Once he figured this out, he quietly went into her bedroom and hid in the closet.

Finally, Amber was finished. She headed for her room. As she turned the knob to go in, she heard someone blowing their car horn. She stopped, turned and went to the front door, opened it and looked out. It was Jimbo. She walked out to his car quickly for news about Jake.

"Hi," Jimbo said with a big smile. "Jake will meet you around 10:00 or 10:30 tomorrow morning at the building. No kids will be around at that time. They'll all be in class."

"Ok," Amber said.

"Say, how would you like a milkshake?" he said. "I got me another job; I'm buying."

"I don't feel like going out," Amber said.

"Well, I'll pick them up and bring them back here and we can sit and talk. It's' just around the corner. I'll be back in a few minutes, ok?"

"Ok," Amber said. "See you in a few minutes. I'll leave the door open, you can just come in. I'll probably be in the kitchen."

"Ok," Jimbo said and drove off. Amber went back in the house and into her bedroom and started picking up her clothes to hang up in her closet. She opened the door and was Paul standing there looking straight at her. She started to scream, but he quickly put his hand over her mouth.

"Now you don't want to scream," he said, "cause then I would have to hurt you and you don't want me to do that, do you?" Amber shook her head no. He took his hand away.

"What are you doing here?" she said as she struggled to get loose from him.

Paul ran his hand through her hair and then he said, "Honey, I've given you everything you wanted: a job that pays you good money, you can buy all the drugs you want. You see I know you're on drugs." He smiled as she continually tried to get away from him. "I even got you fixed up with a car, so now you have to be nice to me. I've wanted you since the first time I saw you. You're so beautiful," he said. "You drive me out of my mind."

"You leave me alone," she said twisting and pulling to get away from him.

"Just calm down and relax," he said. "I promise you a sexual experience you'll never forget. You'll really like it. I love you, Amber."

"You leave me alone, you pig!" she screamed.

Paul became very angry. He grabbed her tightly and said with a smile, "I'm going to have you whether you like it or not." He pulled her close to him, grabbed her hair and pulled her head back, then planted his lips on hers trying to kiss her.

Amber bit his lip hard and drew blood as she twisted loose from him. She ran for the door, but he beat her to it. He spun her around and hit her with his fist. She flew backwards and landed on the bed. Before she could move, he held her down and started trying to take her clothes off. He reached up her dress and tore her panties off.

Then he grabbed her blouse and bra trying to tear them off.

As Amber came out of the shock of being punched, she started fighting back with everything she had. She screamed constantly, bit and scratched him, but he wouldn't stop. He finally opened his pants and took out his penis and was fighting to get it in her.

CHAPTER 27

By this time, Jimbo had just come back, got out of the car, walked up and opened the door and went in the house. As he started to go in the kitchen, he heard Amber scream. He dropped the drinks and ran to her bedroom and went in. He saw Paul lying on top of Amber. He went into a rage. Jimbo was very big and tremendously strong. He grabbed Paul, pulled him off Amber and threw him on the floor. Paul got up with his pants down to his knees and threw a hard punch to Jimbo's jaw. The blow didn't affect him. As Paul tried to throw another punch, Jimbo grabbed him, lifted him clear off the floor and threw him through the air across the room. As Paul landed, the back of his head hit the corner of Amber's dresser. The impact killed him instantly.

Amber looked at Paul in anger and shock. She and Jimbo watched his blood running all over the floor. Jimbo shook all over for he knew he had killed him. He looked at Amber as tears came to his eyes, he said, "I didn't mean to hurt him like that. Oh my God, what am I gonna do? What am I gonna do?" He kept shaking.

Amber finally got her head together. She touched Jimbo and said, "It's not your fault. Just stay right here. I'm going to call the police."

The police arrived quickly and ran in the house. Amber was crying as she sat in a chair. One policeman went to her to question her.

Before he could get started, she said, "Somebody please help Jimbo. He's in my bedroom. It was an accident. He was protecting me. The man in my room was raping me and Jimbo stopped him. Please help him. He's like a little boy when he's scared and hurt. Please help him. It's not his fault."

The police entered Amber's bedroom and found Paul's body on the floor. They called for an ambulance. It finally arrived and Paul was pronounced dead at the scene.

"I didn't mean to kill him," Jimbo cried as he sat crying. "I was just trying to stop him from doing bad things to Amber, and he was hitting me. I didn't mean to kill him."

One of the officers, who knew Jimbo, went to him and said, "It's OK, Jimbo, you didn't do anything wrong. Its Ok." Jimbo just nodded his head, and continued to sob.

Amber told the police what happened, in as much detail as she could. Paul's body was taken to the morgue. Kim was in school so Amber decided not to pull her out and tell her anything right then. Kim knew nothing about her working for Paul and the kind of place she worked in.

The police collected whatever they thought they needed for evidence and cleaned up the blood from the floor and the furniture. They sent Jimbo home and then left also. Amber sat for a minute to collect her self. Finally she decided she had better call Mr. Jenkins.

Jenkins was sitting at his desk when his phone rang. "Hello," he said.

"Mr. Jenkins, it's Amber. We had a terrible thing happen. Paul, Vickie's boyfriend, tried to rape me," and she began to cry. "He was killed; it was an accident. My friend, Jimbo was protecting me, he hit Paul causing him to fall and slam his head on the corner of my dresser and he died. The police took him away. I don't know what's going to happen when Vickie gets back from wherever she went."

"Don't worry about it," Jenkins told her. "You just watch every move she makes, and let me know anything that might help us. You just stay calm and everything will work out for us. I'm sure things will," he said again.

"All right," Amber said. "I'll let you know what's happening." She hung up and sat down and began crying again.

Two days passed and Vickie finally returned home. The cabby helped her carry her luggage and two more boxes she had picked up. She went into the house, went straight to the kitchen, grabbed a bottle of bourbon and poured herself a drink. She drank it quickly and poured another and downed it, too. Then she drank out of the bottle — she couldn't get enough. She finally stopped to catch her breath. She picked up the phone and dialed Paul but there was no answer. She hung up and then dialed a second time. Again there was no answer. Where in the hell is he, she thought to herself.

About that time, Amber walked in the door. She went into the kitchen and saw Vickie sitting at the table, still in her traveling clothes and drinking. Amber watched her for a few seconds and decided she would tell her about Paul. Maybe she would get shook up enough to say something stupid that she could tell Mr. Jenkins. Amber had an inner fear of Vickie; she felt that she could be very violent if pushed too far.

She walked slowly toward the table. Vickie looked up and said, "What the hell do you want?"

Amber was quiet for a second and very slowly choosing her words said, "I thought I should tell you about your friend Paul."

"What about him?" Vickie snapped.

Amber, was hesitant again and then said, "He's dead."

Vickie froze, her eyes got big, and then she said with a gasp, "What in the world are you talking about?"

Amber continued, "Some way he got in the house and was hiding in my closet. When I came home and went in my room, he grabbed me and tried to rape me. My friend Jimbo was outside and heard me screaming and rescued me. When he was fighting with Paul, he accidentally killed him."

Vickie stared hard into space. Amber just stood still, not knowing what to do next. Then Vickie let out a blood curdling scream and yelled at the top of her lungs at Amber. "Get the hell out of here, get out, get out!" she screamed.

Amber turned and ran out the door, down the street to her car, and drove away. Vickie, shaking, poured another drink. As she put it to her lips, she suddenly put it down, laid her head on the table and cried uncontrollably.

Vickie was in terrible shock over Paul's death, and as the next couple of days passed she knew she had to get her act together, or she was going to be in real trouble. She had two sealed boxes of cocaine, and with Paul gone, she was going to have to make contact with their down line suppliers to get it to the street peddlers, who would sell it to the kids or whoever was buying. Teenagers were their biggest business. She came up with a plan. She knew Amber worked real late nights, so that was good. The problem was Kim.

Kim finally came home from school. As she headed for her room, Vickie called to her to come in the kitchen. Kim went up to her and stood in the doorway without saying a word. Vickie asked, "Do you think you could stay over your friend's house for a couple of days? I would like to be alone for a while. I need some time by myself."

"I'll find out," Kim said, and left. She went to Rachel's. Her mother answered the door. Kim asked her and she said it would be fine.

Then Vickie made contact with Mitch and told him to come to the house, entering from the alley around 9:00 p.m. She told him how to knock so she would know it was he and Butch.

CHAPTER 28

Meanwhile, at Mr. Jenkins office, he was pacing back and forth. Amber had called and told him about Paul, but he had already heard from his detective, who advised him to just wait and see what unfolds. Jenkins agreed, but he was worried about Amber. He didn't know Amber had been meeting with Jake.

Back at the farm, Jake was putting the final touches on the tractor. It looked really good, he thought. He hadn't had so much fun in a long time. His withdrawal from coke was building because he was out, so he called Jimbo to have Amber set up another meeting at the old building. Jake decided to take the tractor out of the barn.

He drove it around the yard and started enjoying himself. He was really having a lot of fun.

About that time, Ben came home from work. He got excited as he drove up to the house, seeing Jake having the time of his life on that machine. He walked out to the barnyard. Jake stopped when he saw him coming. Ben had a big smile on his face as he asked Jake. "Can I drive it?"

"Sure," Jake said getting off. "It's yours!"

"No," Ben said, "it's yours and mine, if that's ok with you."

"Sure," Jake said. He turned away from Ben to choke back the tears welling up in his eyes. Ben was like a little kid riding around in circles.

Soon Mabel came with the kids and saw Ben and Jake riding around on the tractor. She got out of the car and just watched. "My God," she said, "that thing really runs." She smiled and took the children in the house.

Ben finally came in the house. As he looked back out the door he said, "Can you believe it?" He turned around. "He's got that thing running like a clock. Look how he's got it cherried out.

It looks like new. If my dad were alive today he would be amazed." Ben and Mabel had no idea how bad Jakes drug problem was and that he still had access to it.

A week passed and Vickie decided to check out the big house. After all, Paul was her partner in everything else so the big house had to be hers, now that he's dead. It was late in the afternoon when she called a cab and headed over. As she arrived, she noticed how attractive the place was from the outside. She got out, walked up the long walk to the front door, opened it and went in. As she looked around from the entrance area she saw a large women coming toward her.

"Hello," the woman said, "I'm Bertha. What can I do for you?"

"I'm Paul's partner. Now that he's gone, I just thought I'd come over and see what he's left me. It looks like a nice set up. Are you in charge here?" she asked.

"Yes," Bertha said, "and I'm also the owner now. I don't know anything about any partner."

Vickie became angry and said, "Everything that's Paul's is mine, so what percent is yours?" she said sarcastically.

"All of it," Bertha said. "When we set the place up, I came here with the agreement that I would own half, and if anything ever happened to him, it was all mine. It's in writing."

"Show me the damn paper," Vickie demanded very angrily.

Bertha smiled and said, "Just wait here, I'll be right back."

As Vickie waited, she peeked into a big open door where two men, who had arrived just ahead, of her had gone. She saw tables set up for playing cards. The liquor bar was nice, too. Amber was in the basement getting food and alcohol to set up the bar, so Vickie didn't see her.

Bertha came back. She walked up to Vickie holding the paper in front of her. Vickie reached for it, but Bertha said, "I'll hold it." Vickie was steaming with anger as she read it. There was absolutely no mention of her any place in the contract.

Then Bertha said, "It's about time for you to leave. There's the door." As she turned and walked away.

Vickie left quickly and fumed all the way home. She got out of the cab, stomped up to the door and went in. She headed straight for the kitchen, sat down and poured a small drink. She knew she couldn't drink too much, since she expected to meet with Mitch and Butch. It was about 9:00 p.m. when she heard the signal knock she has given them. She opened the door and they came in.

"Sit down," she said, "I'll get the stuff." She came back with a large box. She opened it and showed them the small packets of cocaine.

"How much?" Mitch asked.

"Ten thousand," she said.

"Ten thousand!" he said, a little shocked.

"The price has gone up," Vickie said. "Come on you guys... you'll make a fortune and you know it."

"But all I got is six," he said.

"You're short," she said.

"I got a guy who owes us four," he said, "but we're having a hard time collecting."

Vickie quickly replied, "Hey, that's not my problem. If you want the stuff, go collect it and come back."

"Well, the guy just got out of jail," Mitch told her. "He meets your daughter Amber down at the old building by the high school."

"No, I don't know that," Vickie said angrily. "Do you have a gun?"

"Yeah," Mitch said.

"How about you?" she asked Butch.

"Yeah, Butch said.

"Then scare him," she said. "Scare him so bad he'll go out and rob a couple of liquor stores or a bank or something. But no coke until I get the bucks."

Butch and Mitch just looked at each other, shrugged their shoulders, and started to leave. Vickie said, "Wait a minute," then she paused a moment like she was in deep thought. "I want you to keep an eye on Amber for me at the same time. Let me know what she's doing, Ok?"

"Sure," Mitch said as they went out the door. They got in their car and Mitch went to start the engine when he stopped and just stared ahead.

"Come on, let's go," Butch said.

"Just a minute, I'm thinking," Mitch replied. Finally he said, "You know, if we just follow Amber around, she'll lead us to Jake. We won't have to sit around and guess when he's coming."

"Yeah, that's a good idea," said Butch, who wasn't too bright.

The next day Mitch and Butch parked about a block away from the front of Amber's house. They were about halfway between her house and the old building by the school. Looking across an open field from where they were parked, they could see her front door. Vickie had told them about the time Amber usually left. Finally, they saw her coming out the door. They watched as she turned and walked down the sidewalk until she was out of sight.

Mitch drove slowly forward until he got up close to the end of the block and they could see her again. They watched her walk across the street and as she was getting into her car. They waited until she drove away and then followed her, staying far behind. Amber reached the big house, parked, and went in. They waited a minute, then parked and decided to go in. They didn't know that Amber knew who they were. They walked in the door, looked around and then looked in the bar and card room. They saw Amber behind the bar setting up the glasses and food snack dishes, then turned and left. Amber didn't see them.

Mitch called Vickie from a pay phone and said when Vickie answered, "It's me, Mitch. We followed your girl. She went to that place Paul used to run, called the big house. She works there."

Vickie was stunned. "Are you sure it was her? She doesn't drive; she doesn't even have a car."

"Hey, we followed her from your house and she has a car and drives. It was her," he said.

Vickie just hung up without answering. She was steaming. How did she get a car? She's not old enough to own a car. Vickie wanted to kill Amber. She blamed her for Paul's death, but down deep in her spirit she knew better. She knew Paul's weaknesses. She knew she had to play it cool for a while till the boys collected their money from her boyfriend. But inside she boiled with such hatred for Amber over Paul's death. She was convinced Amber alone was responsible for causing Paul to go off the deep end.

CHAPTER 29

The next day rolled around. Today was the day Amber was to meet Jake at the old building, and she always got a little excited when she knew she was going to see him.

Mitch and Butch were parked at the same place they were yesterday, only they didn't have to wait long. It was still morning when Amber came out the door and headed down the street to her car. She had no idea that Vickie knew she had a car. As Amber walked down the street, Mitch and Butch drove forward slowly to keep her in sight. She got in her car, put her key in the ignition and turned it. The car wouldn't start. It just made noises like it was trying to, but just wouldn't start. She did it over and over until she ran the battery down.

She was starting to become anxious because she knew Jake would be at the meeting place soon. Then she was beginning to panic. She needed to get to a phone, she thought, but she couldn't go back to the house because Vickie was at home . She decided to walk down to the malt shop, just a couple of blocks away and use a pay phone. As she walked, the two men followed cautiously. They parked and watched her make a phone call. She had called an auto repair shop; they told her they would send a man out to check her car.

She hung up and started walking back to her car. The men saw her coming, but couldn't turn the car around from where they parked without risking she would see them. So they slid down low in the seat so she wouldn't see they were there. After she passed, they drove down the street and turned around, and slowly followed her till she reached her car. They parked their car and watched her. Soon a repair truck showed up. The driver got out of his truck and asked Amber to pull the lever to open her hood, as he pulled cables from his truck. He hooked them to her battery and said, "There's an automatic service charge of forty-five dollars just for driving out here, plus whatever it costs to fix it. Do you have the money to pay me?" The repairman saw that she was just a kid, and didn't want to take the chance of not getting paid.

"I don't know," Amber said. She dug in her purse and came up with about fifty dollars. She said, "I only have enough to pay for your coming, but if you'll fix it, I'll run home and get some more money. I don't live far from here."

"All right," he said. "I'll at least try to find out what's wrong till you get back." She began walking very fast, sometimes running, to get home quickly. Time was passing by and she was going to be late meeting Jake. She reached her house and went straight in to her room. She saw Vickie sitting at the table drinking as usual.

Mitch and Butch saw her disappear into the house. "Well," Mitch said, "we know where to find her. Let's drive over and take a peek and see if Jake has showed up."

They went to the old building and drove around the block to the backside, stopping at the turn going into the alley. Sure enough, the old pickup was parked: he was there. They left their car and walked up the alley to the old building. Very quietly, they peeked through cracks in the wood and walls. They finally spotted him sitting on an old crate waiting for Amber.

Mitch whispered to Butch, "Do you have your gun on you?"

"Yeh," Butch answered.

"Let's scare him," said Mitch. "You sneak around behind him and stick your gun in his back and then I'll come out holding mine. That oughta scare the hell out of him."

Butch snuck around behind Jake and stuck his gun in his back and said, "Get your hands up." Jake raised his hands in shock as Mitch approached him then from the front, holding his gun pointing down at the floor.

"Well, well, well," Mitch said, smiling. "Who have we here? Are you waiting for someone?"

Jake just looked at him with fear in his eyes and said, "What do you want?"

"You know what we want," Mitch replied. "Where's our money, four thousand bucks, remember?"

"I haven't got it," Jake said. "I just got out of honor camp. I'm on probation."

"I don't care about that," Mitch said. "Where's our money?" he repeated.

"The cops took it when I was arrested. I can't get it back."

"Then how you gonna pay it back?" Mitch asked, pressing his gun into Jake's stomach.

"I don't know," Jake said. "I'll need some time to figure it out."

"You don't have any time," Mitch responded angrily.

As Jake and Mitch talked, Amber had run home and found some more money in a hiding place inside her closet. She grabbed it, and ran out the door all the way down the street to her car. She was out of breath when she got back.

As she was panting she asked, "Did you find the problem?"

"No," the mechanic said. "I'm going to have to tow it in. It seems to be some kind of electrical problem. I need to put it on a scope to find it."

"All right," she said. He gave her some papers to sign. After that, she took off running up the street and down another block to the other side of the old building, where she saw Mitch's car parked. She wondered whose it belonged to. She could see Jake's truck up the alley in back of the building. She decided to walk up quietly to see what was going on. She got close, peeked through a crack in the wall, and saw Butch and Mitch. They both had guns. She was frightened. She heard Mitch demand the four thousand dollars. Then she remembered the money she found hidden in Vickie's drawer, in a box. She decided to take a chance. She would go get the money and deal with Vickie later. Right now she had to save Jake. She walked softly for a few minutes and then took off running for home. She rushed in, saw Vickie passed out at the table, ran in Vickie's room hurrying, but trying to be as quiet as she could. She opened the drawer, found the box, opened it and took the money. She slipped out of the house and hurried back to the old building.

The bell rang across the street at the high school. It was lunchtime and the students were coming out.

Mitch had pushed Jake to the point of panic. Jake knew how ruthless these guys were. He didn't know what he was going to do. Then he looked out the door and saw the kids coming out of school, in the streets and sidewalk. He decided to make a break for it. He pushed Mitch back and out the door. Butch quickly fired his gun twice, hitting Jake in the neck and back as he fled. Jake staggered and fell in the middle of the street. The students were screaming and yelling, some of them dropped to the ground while others tried to hide behind trees and bushes. No one saw the direction the shots came from.

Kim and Rachel were in the second floor classroom just hanging out as usual. They were always the last ones to get their stuff together. When they heard the shots, they rushed to the windows, but couldn't see what happened. They saw kids running, screaming, and looking for someplace to hide. It was a long way from the front door of the school to the street and the landscaping was wooded with a lot of bushes. Because of that, the view from where the two girls were was very limited. Rachel said, "I think we ought to stay inside for a while," looking a little frightened.

"I think you're right," Kim said, and they both stepped back away from the windows.

Mitch yelled at Butch, "You stupid son-of-a-bitch! Why did you shoot him? We were just going to scare him you dumb ass. Come on, we got to get lost, quick."

As they started out the back door they saw a patrol car with two officers, looking at their car that was illegally parked. They went back in the building. Mitch said, "Look, we'll go out the front and mix in with the crowd." They were gathering around Jake's body, mostly students and teachers. Some were seeing what they could do to help. The police and ambulance had already been called.

They put their guns away and slowly walked out the door and maneuvered through the crowd to get close to Jake to see if he was dead.

Finally Amber reached the back of the building. She never heard the shots. She rushed in, but no one was inside. She saw all the people standing in the middle of the street, and went to the door. She didn't see Jake anywhere. She ran out and pushed through the crowd to find Jake. His truck was still there, so he had to be somewhere. As she pushed through the people, she saw Jake lying on the ground with blood all around him. She screamed and rushed to him, kneeling down, screaming and crying, "Jake, Jake."

As she knelt there, two policemen finally maneuvered through the crowd and got to Jake. Amber looked up, screaming for help, and saw Butch and Mitch, standing in the crowd watching her. She jumped up and ran to them crying hysterically, "Here, here, here's your money," as she pulled the money out of a cloth bag she was carrying. "You didn't have to shoot him," she screamed as she shoved some of the money in Butch's chest and then some more in Mitch's stomach. "See, I got the money," she screamed again as she pulled out some more money and threw it at them. The two police officers started taking their guns out; Butch panicked and he turned and started running towards the old building pulling his gun out. Mitch panicked, He knew they were exposed and in real troubled so he ran for the building as well.

CHAPTER 30

The crowd panicked and the people started running, screaming and looking for a safe place to hide. As they reached the door, one of the policemen yelled, "Halt! Drop your guns!"

Butch turned and fired his gun. Mitch knew it was do or die so he fired too. The police jumped behind a car close to where they were and returned the fire. As Mitch pulled the door shut, they kept shooting back through the holes and cracks in the door. In the alley, the two officers who were looking at their car heard the shooting. They ran up the alley and when they got close to the building, they slowed down and cautiously approached the back entrance that had no door. They looked in and saw Butch and Mitch shooting out the front door.

One officer signaled to the other and then yelled, "Drop your guns now or we will shoot."

Butch and Mitch both turned and fired at them. Both officers fired back shooting several times. Mitch and Butch dropped to the floor, bleeding badly. They were killed almost instantly. The officers approached them cautiously to make sure they were dead.

While all this was going, Amber was down on her knees, holding Jake's head in her lap. The two officers who were hiding behind their car came out. One went toward the old building to communicate with the two officers inside. The other officer headed toward Amber as the ambulance drove up. The crowd slowly started coming back. Amber sat on the ground crying and talking to Jake. "It's going to be ok, honey, just hang on. The ambulance is here. I'm here, honey, it's going to be all right."

The paramedic knelt down by Amber and checked Jake's pulse. He looked at Amber, very caring, and softly said, "I'm sorry, but he's dead. I'm sorry," he repeated.

Amber went into shock. "He's not dead," she screamed, "He's not dead. Check him again," she said as the policeman and one of the paramedics got her hands free of Jake, and took her over by the squad car. She cried, out of control, as the paramedic gave her a shot to help calm her down. The officer helped her into the back seat of his car. He then went over to Jake's body. All the policemen had arrived, trying to calm the people and get everything under control the best they could. Amber watched the ambulance take Jake away.

The officer came back to his car, got in, turned, looked at Amber and asked. "Where do you live, Ms?" Amber told him and he drove away. Amber was in a daze, she felt numb all over. She was as depressed as a person could be. Her mind was blank and she felt like her life was over. What was she going to do without Jake? He was her whole life. She cried quietly as the policeman drove her home.

At home, Vickie had sobered up enough to get up and go to the bathroom. As she came out, she noticed the door to her room was opened. She never left it like that, so she went in and looked around. She saw the drawer open where she kept her money hidden. She went over, reached in and moved stuff around till she found her moneybox. It was open and empty. She knew Amber had taken it since Vickie had caught Amber in her room before. Vickie screamed and said, "I'll kill the bitch, so help me, I'm going to kill her." She looked in a lower drawer, reached way back in it and pulled out a gun and stuck it in her pocket. She staggered back to the kitchen, poured herself another drink and sat down.

She fell asleep for a while, then woke up hearing the doorbell ring. She got up and staggered to the door. She straightened her clothes a little, brushed her hair with her fingers, and then opened the door. When she saw a policeman standing there with Amber, she almost panicked, but managed to keep her cool.

"What's the matter?" she asked.

"Mrs. Colden?" the officer asked.

"Yes," Vickie answered.

"I brought your daughter home. She's pretty shook up. Her boyfriend was shot and killed by a couple of drug dealers. It apparently was over money, from what we saw and heard. They were both killed when they decided to shoot it out rather than give up. We'll come and question her in a few days when she's feeling better."

He turned and left. Amber went in her room, threw herself on the bed and began crying again. Vickie staggered back to the kitchen in shock. She knew it was Butch and Mitch that were killed. She didn't know what to do. They were her best and biggest customers for drugs.

Paul's dead, now they're dead, her whole business was falling apart. She thought she might run, but then she remembered, Amber took all her money. That really angered her. She sat down and had another drink, and the more she thought about her money being gone, the madder she got.

Meanwhile, Kim and Rachel eventually decided it was safe enough to come out of the school and go home. They couldn't see much of what had happened, so Kim didn't know Amber was involved in the shooting or anything else that went on.

As they walked out, Kim said, "I've got to go by the house and pick up some things I forgot. Do you want to go with me?" she asked.

"Sure!" Rachel said. So they walked happily down the street.

Back at the house, Vickie poured herself another drink. As she sat there, all of a sudden her anger and frustration peaked and panic set in. She got up and walked to the sink, turned around and just shook. She took another drink. She didn't have Paul to lean on or tell her what to do. Then her thoughts switched to Amber. In her mind Amber was the cause and she was going to pay. She couldn't wait to see how John's will was going to turn out. There was no more time. That bitch has been the pain in my ass since John died. If I'm going down, I'm going to take her with me. She was scared. All of a sudden Vickie screamed, "Amber, get your ass out here." The drug they gave Amber was starting to wear off and she heard Vickie. Then Vickie yelled again. "Did you hear me? Get out here." Amber got up and walked slowly to the door, opened it and walked into the kitchen. The kitchen was large so she kept her distance.

"Whatta you want?" she said, her voice just a little above a whisper.

"I want my money back," Vickie said very loudly.

"I haven't got it," Amber replied.

"Where is it?" Vickie yelled.

"I gave it to the two guys who shot Jake. The police probably have it now." Vickie's panic grew more and her temper was getting out of control as Amber continued. "And you know what? I don't give a damn," as she took two steps toward Vickie to show she wasn't afraid of her.

Amber continued to attacked Vickie verbally. She didn't care anymore and wanted to hurt her.

"I know you work at the whore house Paul started and you have a car," Vickie snapped as Amber moved towards her.

"Your boyfriend Paul signed for me," Amber said, knowing that would really get to her.

Vickie yelled, "How many times did you have to go to bed with him for that? What did you do? Cut him off when your boyfriend got outa prison, and then scream rape when he came after you, you little bitch."

"I never let him touch me," Amber yelled back. "He was a slime bag. He was a pig, do you hear me, a pig. I couldn't stomach being around him."

Then Amber, because of her own anger, exposed what was going on. She took more steps toward Vickie and said, "The cops have been watching you and Paul for a long time, just waiting for you to screw up. And you know what? I helped them. I was nice to Paul so you and he would play right into their hands. They're really going to get you."

Fear and panic took control of Vickie. She pulled the gun out of her pocket and pointed it at Amber. "You slut," she said, hardly able to talk. "If I go down you're going with me."

When Amber saw the gun, she got scared. "Don't, don't," she said as she took a step backwards. Vickie fired, hitting Amber in the chest. She fired again hitting her in the stomach. Amber fell to the floor and she was bleeding badly. As the second shot was fired, Kim came through the door with Rachel right behind her. When she saw Amber fall to the floor, she screamed and ran towards Vickie, grabbing her arm and struggling to get control of the gun. Rachel turned and ran out the door and down the street, heading for her house, screaming and crying. The only thing she knew was to go and get her dad.

Kim and Vickie struggled over the gun, spinning around and bouncing off the cabinets, walls and chairs. As Amber was lying on the floor, she was semi conscious. Her eyes were blurry, then clear. Then Vickie and Kim fell to the floor and the gun flew out of Vickie's hand and slid across the floor close to Amber. Amber saw it and struggled to reach it, but she was extremely weak. She had lost a lot of blood. Vickie was desperately trying to get loose from Kim and get her gun back. But Kim was very strong even though she wasn't as big as Vickie. They both got up from the floor. Amber was still trying to reach the gun. Amber finally got her hands on it, her eyes were blurred again and she was so weak.

Rachel finally reached her house, running in screaming and crying "DAD, DAD." He came running out of his office, calmed her down as she told him what happened. They both ran out of the house, heading for Kim's, with Beverly right behind them.

CHAPTER 31

Meanwhile, Kim and Vickie were still fighting. They were both getting exhausted and they fell to the floor again. Vickie fell on top of Kim and Kim's head hit the floor hard knocking her senseless for a few seconds. Vickie struggled to get up and her eyes caught sight of the knife rack on the counter. She staggered as she got up to get to it, pulled out a butcher knife, and then staggered towards Kim. Then, Amber's eyes focused again and she saw Vickie standing over Kim, raising the knife to stab her. She aimed the gun the best she could. She was very weak, but she managed to pull the trigger. The bullet hit Vickie in the temple. She was killed instantly and fell to the floor.

Kim was regaining consciousness. She sat up and saw Vickie lying on the floor, with her eyes open. She turned as Amber dropped the gun and crawled to her, crying, "Amber, Amber." She knelt and pulled her sister up in her lap. "Amber," she cried, "please don't die. Hang on please until help comes."

Even in her pain, Amber gave Kim a slight smile. "I won't leave you," she said as she could barely talk. "I can't leave you; I've got to take care of you. You're my baby sister. Don't worry, I'll be ok. I'm just so tired and cold. I think if I just sleep for a little while, I'll be all right." Her head rolled off to one side as the life went out of her. She was dead.

Kim cried hysterically, "Amber, Amber." Pastor Harding burst into the room with Rachel. He knelt down and closed Amber's eyes. He gently took Amber out of Kim's lap and then slowly helped her get up. Kim saw Rachel and grabbed her and hugged her tightly as she cried, out of control. Beverly finally arrived and helped Rachel walk Kim outside.

By that time, the police showed up and went inside. Pastor Harding filled them in the best he could. Then he asked them to please not question Kim at that time until she got over the shock. They agreed.

Kim looked up at Pastor Harding as he approached her, "Would you call Mr. Jenkins?" she said through her tears.

"I sure will," he said. Then he motioned for Beverly to take Kim to their home. Beverly nodded and she and Rachel helped Kim down the steps to the sidewalk.

As they reached the house to go in, Rachel said, "Mother, I want to go in the church and pray."

"All right," Beverly said. Then she helped Kim to Rachel's room.

Rachel went into the sanctuary, walked down and knelt at the altar. She looked up at a picture of Christ hanging on the wall. She wept softly and said, "Lord, I thank you for everything you've done in my life. But what about Kim? Why does she have to suffer so? I don't know if I could bear the pain she's had to live with. She lost both her mother and father, and now her sister. The tragedy she's had to suffer I just don't understand."

At that moment she felt a hand on her shoulders. She looked up; her father was standing there and he knelt down beside her. "Honey," he said, "the Bible says we live in a world that is imperfect, full of sin, and only through God can we survive it. Without Him we will succumb to it and it will destroy us. He can use our suffering and pain to help grow us up to be strong and faithful, with wisdom and understanding because we've experienced difficulties. When you grow up and get married, have children of your own, you will have the knowledge to help them, so hopefully they don't have to suffer like you did. You learn how to love instead of hate, have understanding, to use wisdom in your walk through the life we've been given. Instead of walking around blindly, following other people into disaster, we can live a more productive life in this cruel world. If we have love, wisdom, understanding and forgiveness in our hearts, we can endure more pain. God is always faithful, if we just have patience. He operates on his timetable, not ours. We just have to trust him."

Rachel smiled through the tears and said, "Thanks, Daddy. I'm ok now." They both went back into the house. Rachel went to her room to help comfort Kim. Pastor Harding went in his office, looked up Mr. Jenkins' phone number, and called him.

Mr. Jenkins was just about ready to leave his office when the phone rang. He picked it up and said, "Hello."

"Mr. Jenkins, This is Pastor Harding. I've got some very bad news for you. We've had a catastrophe on our side of town. I'm sorry to have to tell you that Amber Colden is dead. Her step-mother shot her."

Mr. Jenkins was stunned as he listened to the Pastor tell him everything that happened. When he told Jenkins that Vickie was dead and how she died, he was horrified. He sat down in his chair as he hung up. His knees were weak and he shook all over; he sat there just feeling numb. He took out his handkerchief and wiped the cold sweat from his face. His phone rang again. He was afraid to answer but it kept ringing and finally he picked it up.

It was the private investigator, Jordan Willis. "Are you sitting down Dave?"

"Oh no," said Jenkins, "what's happened now?"

"That kid, Jake Moran, the one who was paroled to you..."

"Yes," Jenkins said slowly.

"Well he's dead. He was shot by those two creeps he owed all that money to. You know the ones we've been trying to track — Mitch and Butch. I don't know what their real names are."

"What happened to them?" Jenkins asked.

"They're dead," Willis said. "They shot it out with the police down by the high school, by that old building."

Jenkins was drained mentally.

"Hello!" Willis repeated. "Are you still there?"

"Yes," Jenkins said slowly. "I guess that blows our whole investigation to pieces."

"Well, not really," Willis said, "we've tracked Vickie through the cab company where she made her pick up. They got a warrant, just in case they have to move fast. Now that Vickie and Paul are dead, it won't surprise me if they hit that place tomorrow. So we didn't do too badly." Willis said bye and hung up. Jenkins was so numb he just sat there staring into space for about fifteen minutes, then finally got up and went home.

Back at the farm, Ben had gotten home a little earlier than usual. He got out of his car and looked around, walking toward the house. Then he stopped and decided to go see how Jake was coming with the paint job on the tractor. He entered the barn but nobody was there. He noticed the tractor was done. It really looked good. He yelled, "Jake, where are you?"

There was no answer. He yelled again, "Jake," but there still was no answer. He looked out the back door of the barn, but no Jake. Then he noticed the old truck was gone. Oh no, he thought, I hope he hasn't done anything stupid. He walked around and looked in all the other sheds. He went into the little cabin that Jake was living. He looked all around, but didn't find anything that would give him a clue where Jake was.

As he was coming out, he saw Mabel driving in with the kids. He walked toward them feeling very depressed. He was beginning to really like Jake and the fact he was missing disturbed him. As he reached the car, Mabel knew something was wrong by the look on his face. "What's the matter?" she asked, as she was getting out of her car.

"Jake's gone," he said, disgusted. "He took the old truck. It's not licensed. If a cop stops him he'll be right back in the honor camp or worse. God, why did he do that?" Ben said dejectedly.

Mabel knew Ben was really starting to like Jake a lot and she felt so bad for him. She put her hand on his arm and said, "Maybe it won't be as bad as we think it is. Maybe he got a call from Jenkins."

"No," Ben said, "he wouldn't have taken the truck." Mabel said no more and took the kids into the house.

The shock was starting to wear off as Jenkins got home. His mind was in gear and working again. He grabbed the phone and called Ben and Mabel. Mabel answered the phone. "This is Mr. Jenkins," he said. "Can I talk to Ben?"

"Sure," she said. "It's for you, Ben," and handed him the phone. Mabel suddenly got a chill and knew something was really wrong. She watched Ben intently.

"Hello," Ben said.

"Ben," Jenkins said, "I'm sorry to tell you, but Jake was shot and killed today by a couple of drug dealers he owed money to. Jake had a girl friend named Amber. I just found out she was meeting him at different times to supply him with drugs when he needed them." Jenkins voice shook. "She was a good girl. I've known her and her family for a long time. They are all deceased except for her younger sister Kim."

Ben was stunned. As Jenkins talked, a tear ran down his cheek. Mabel saw it and started crying quietly. She knew something terrible had happened. Ben hung up the phone, looked at

Mabel and said in a shaky voice, "I was really getting to like that kid. I really was." Then he got up and went into another room to be by himself for a few moments.

Mabel was still crying quietly as the children kept asking her what was wrong. She finally looked at them and said. Jake won't be coming back to live with us any more. Her daughter started crying, "But I like Jake. Why doesn't he want to live with us?"

Mabel put her hand on her cheek and said, "I don't know, honey, but I'm sure he's much happier now. I'm sure it's very peaceful where he is at now."

The next morning when Kim woke and got out of bed, she ached all over and her head hurt. Beverly took her to a doctor to check her over and make sure she was all right. When they got back, Pastor Harding told Kim that he made all the arrangements for Amber's funeral. He also informed Mr. Jenkins. Mr. Jenkins also got in touch with Ben and Mabel to say he had made arrangements with Pastor Harding for Jake's funeral, and they agreed that would be fine.

CHAPTER 32

As Kim sat very quiet in the living room she suddenly asked Beverly, "What's going to happen to me?"

"We'll have to call Mr. Jenkins," Beverly said and looked at her husband. He knew what she was thinking and nodded yes with approval.

Mr. Harding said, "I'll call Mr. Jenkins and make an appointment." He went in his office and closed the door. He dialed Jenkins' office. Jenkins came to the phone. Pastor Harding said he was calling to make an appointment for Kim to come in to see him, but he wanted to first meet with Jenkins before bringing Kim to see him. He said that he and Beverly had something concerning Kim they would like to discuss with him as soon as possible. Mr. Jenkins agreed, and a time was set.

As Pastor Harding hung up and started for the door, the phone rang. He picked it up; it was one of the board members of the church. He informed him that his replacement would be arriving sooner than they thought, and he could prepare to leave in a couple of weeks. Pastor Harding's heart jumped with joy for at good news. He hung up and quickly went in the living room.

"Bev, Rachel, we'll be moving in a couple of weeks, my replacement will be here."

"That's wonderful," Beverly said, looking at the girls. Neither Rachel nor Kim showed any emotion. They just looked at each other with a sad smile. Beverly understood and said nothing.

Pastor Harding then said, "Mr. Jenkins will let us know when to bring you to his office, Kim."

He continued, "When you're able, Kim, you and Rachel can go up to your house and get some more of your things you need and you can continue to stay with us. There's no sense you staying in that house alone, especially after what's happened. I don't think you want to do that, do you?"

"No," Kim said, "no."

When the police finished gathering all the evidence of Vickie's drug operation and death, they allowed a house cleaning company to come in and clean the place up. The next morning, as Kim and Rachel were getting ready to go and get some more of Kim's things from the house, Pastor Harding informed Kim the funeral for Amber would be on Sunday after church. He also told her Mr. Jenkins had asked him to take care of Jake's funeral also. He thought it would be good to have Jake buried by his mother. Kim had no idea what they did with Vickie's body, and she really didn't care.

Kim and Rachel reached the house. Rachel went in but Kim hesitated, a little fear setting in, sort of like a nightmare while still awake. Finally she went in. A chill went through her as she went through the door. She peeked in Vickie's room and saw it was stripped of everything except the bed and dresser. She went to her room, which looked the same as it did the last time she was in it. She went in the kitchen and looked around. She got a chill again as she went out the back door. She went around the corner of the porch where Mollie's dog house was, bent down and took Mollie's collar off the rope and looked at her name engraved in the brass identity plate. A small tear trickled down her cheek as she thought how she missed her little dog. Then under her breath, she said, "I love you, Mollie, wherever you are."

She went back in the house to her room. She got all the things she thought she needed and left. As they walked in the door of Rachel's house, Kim started thinking about the funeral for her sister. Something struck her mind. Where are they going to bury Vickie? She could not tolerate her being buried anywhere near her mother and father.

She went to see Pastor Harding. "Pastor, can I talk to you?"

"Yes," he said, "what's on your mind?"

"Well," Kim hesitated, "I don't want Vickie buried near my parents. She has no right to be there. She used my father and trapped him when he was very lonely."

"All right," he said. "We'll make sure that doesn't happen."

Kim was still feeling overwhelmed with grief so she walked outside and just started wandering around in a daze, very depressed.

All of a sudden she realized she was back in the little park she used to go to with her father. She saw the bench they would sometimes sit and talk. Her mind reminisced back about the fun times they had. He would tell her about her mother who she never really knew because she died when Kim was very small. They used to talk and laugh. They were so happy. Then reality set in. She started thinking of the things that had happened over the last few months. She never felt so alone as she did at that moment. She started crying. Her heart ached so badly, it was difficult to breathe. She didn't know what was going to happen to her. As she got up and started walking back to Rachel's, she looked up to the sky and cried out, " God!

God, if you can hear me , please help me, please!" As she sobbed.

Sunday morning came. After the morning service was over, they had a service for Amber. As Kim sat listening to Pastor Harding speak, she found herself lost in an almost paradox of numb pain. She just kept praying for the strength to get through the day. Later, at the cemetery, Kim watched as they lowered Amber's casket into the grave. Tears flowed down her face. Once the casket was released at the bottom, Kim threw the flowers she was holding on top and said, "Goodbye, Amber...I love you, I miss you and I'll never forget you. I promise."

A few hours later, another funeral was held for Jake. Kim never knew Jake, but she went to his funeral because she felt that's what Amber would want her to do. As Pastor Harding stood at his grave, before they lowered Jake's body, he said, "I feel so sorry for this boy. He never had a chance in life to find himself. He did some bad things, but he did them out of desperation, because he had no father to guide and help him to take care of his mother. This is such a catastrophe. He had a good heart, but got involved with the wrong people and they used him. It tears my heart out when I have to speak over our young people as they're laid in the ground. Nearly all their deaths are related to drugs in one way or another. I pray that God will give us the courage to answer this devastation with a commitment to change. It's heart breaking. Lord, please help us. Amen."

Ben and Mabel both shed tears as Jake was laid, to rest beside his mother. After Mr. Jenkins watched them lower Jake's body, he turned to Ben and said, "You know, if the Middle East was smart they would realize they don't have to make bombs to destroy us. If they would just lay back and wait, we'll destroy ourselves with drugs. Then they can just walk in and take over."

He shook his head as he walked away. Then he turned and went back to Ben, reached in his pocket, and handed him a piece of paper. It was from the police department giving him the right to pick up his old truck from the city impound. Ben thanked him and then said, "You know, under different circumstances, I think Jake could have turned out to be a good man."

"Well," Jenkins said, "if you had said that to me a year ago, I would have disagreed with you. But now, looking back, and seeing what's happened to Amber, I agree with you. Under different circumstances they both probably would have turned out pretty good."

Jenkins reached out and shook his hand and said, "I'll see you. If you ever need an attorney, give me a call." He smiled and went on his way.

Rachel continued going to school with Kim until they were ready to leave. Rachel and Kim made plans to write and keep in touch. They had become such close friends, it saddened them, that soon they wouldn't see each other for a long time.

CHAPTER 33

A week later, it was time for Pastor Harding to have his meeting with Mr. Jenkins. He had Beverly go with him. They went in and sat down in Jenkins office.

"What can I do for you?" Jenkins asked.

They looked at each other and Pastor Harding spoke. "We were wondering if there was any way Kim could come and live with us. We have seen how close the girls have become over the last year. You would think they were sisters. Bev and I have become very attached to her. She doesn't deserve to be put in a foster home or live with another relative she doesn't even know. She's not even sure if there are any relatives. I have accepted a position at a new church, and she would not be a financial burden at all. We hate to separate them. I have a good feeling this is what the Lord would want us to do."

Jenkins didn't say anything as he watched them for a few moments. Then he smiled and said, "I think that's a great idea. We could work it out with the courts and she would be in your custody until she's of age. You don't have to worry about her financially, her father left the girls well fixed. With Amber gone now, it's all Kim's."

Pastor Harding and Beverly both looked a little surprised. Then Jenkins said, "I have a meeting Saturday morning with Kim. Let's see," he said as he looked at the calendar, "that's tomorrow! I'm presuming you and your wife, are planning to bring her in. Why don't all of you come? Let's not tell her anything yet. When you come in, send her into my office first while you wait in the other room. I'll get some personal stuff settled and then I'll call you in and will present the idea to her."

Saturday morning came. They had breakfast and were getting ready to take Kim to see Mr. Jenkins. Rachel noticed her mom and dad seemed a little nervous and excited. Finally she looked at her mom and said, "Mom, what's going on, why are you so fidgety this morning?"

She looked at her a little surprised and said, "Really, I am?"

"Yes," Rachel said, not taking her eyes off her mother.

"Well," Beverly said, "I guess it's just everything that's going on...us moving and Kim being taken care of..." Rachel accepted that and went back to her room to get ready to go.

They arrived at Jenkins' office and went in. As Kim started into Jenkins' private office, she noticed that Rachel and her parents just sat down. "Aren't you going in with me?" she asked.

"No," Beverly answered, "we'll wait out here."

Kim went in and sat down in a chair across from Mr. Jenkins.

"Well," Mr. Jenkins said, "hold on to your seat. I've got a lot of stuff for you to sign. With Vickie out of the picture, and, I'm sorry to say, Amber gone too, everything goes to you." Kim just stared at Mr. Jenkins, so he continued. "Your dad had a Life Insurance policy that will give you about two-hundred, fifty thousand dollars." Kim's eyes almost jumped out of her head. "Then," Jenkins continued, "he had another policy that would pay you girls two thousand dollars a month until you're twenty-one years of age. In case of his death his mortgage insurance paid off the house, so that's yours free and clear. He really looked out for you girls," he went on. "The house is probably worth about one hundred and fifty thousand, but I don't think you ought to sell it right away, because the market's going to go up, and as young as you are, some day it will be worth at least double what it is now."

Kim was numb. She was totally overwhelmed with all of he was saying. She could hardly speak. Mr. Jenkins just smiled. He got up went to the door and motioned with his hand for the Hardings to come in. They all sat down.

Mr. Jenkins said, "Kim, Mr. and Mrs. Harding have asked if you could go to live with them."

Rachel almost jumped out of her chair. Her eyes got real big as the tears of joy came. Kim jumped with joy and hugged Beverly and Pastor Harding. She turned to Rachel grabbed her and hugged her, too. They were speechless.

As they settled down, Mr. Jenkins, with a big smile on his face, continued. "I don't think there will be any problems with the judge. I'll get busy on the paperwork on Monday. I don't think it will take more than a couple of days to iron out the details."

The next week passed very slowly for the girls. They were so excited about the move and their future. It was just a couple more days before they were planning to leave. Kim felt a deep need to go to the cemetery and take one last look at the graves of her family. Rachel asked Kim if she wanted her to go along.

"No," Kim said, "I want to be alone with them."

"Sure," Rachel said. "I understand."

Kim stopped and got some flowers, then went to the cemetery. She knelt down and laid some flowers on her mother's grave first. "I'm sorry, Mommy, that I never got to know you better. You left when I was so young, but I will never forget you. I remember how pretty you were. Daddy used to say I looked so much like you, so I'll always have an image of you."

Then she got up and moved over and knelt at her father's grave. She laid some flowers on it and the tears came. "Oh, Daddy, why did you have to leave me? I need you so much." She cried for a minute and then got her composure back. "I'm going to live with my friend Rachel. She's sort of my sister now that Amber has gone to be with you and Mom. I'll come back and talk to you now and then. I won't ever forget you."

Then she moved over to Amber's grave and the tears came again. "Oh Amber, I wish you were here. I wish I could have been able to help you. I know you're at peace now; I just miss you so much." She laid the rest of the flowers on her grave and got up and said, "Lord, please take good care of them. I love them so much." She turned and started to walk away, stopped, looked down at a small grave near her father. Bye Molly. I won't ever forget you either. With her goodbyes done, she slowly made her way back to Rachel's house.

It was Friday morning and everyone was up early getting the Suburban and trailer packed with all their personal belongings. A moving van would bring their furniture. They took one look around and got in the car. As they drove slowly away, they passed by the cemetery. Kim looked out across in the direction her family was buried. Under her breath she said, "Goodbye. I'll never forget you." She would come back to visit them some day, but she knew she would never live in that town again. There were just too many heart-felt sorrows. She turned and looked ahead to the new life she was beginning.

THE END

Breinigsville, PA USA
26 September 2010
246112BV00003B/2/P